THE INCREDIBLE LIFE OF WILLIE SHARP ACT 2

THE INCREDIBLE LIFE OF WILLIE SHARP ACT 2

Saved by John Da' Pope

A NOVEL BY
ROBERT THURSTON HANKINS JR.

RTH Publishing.

Contents

This book is dedicated to
The memory of
Tyrone Jones
And Ed Roe
And to the people of North Oakland.

Book Design by Robert Thurston Hankins Jr.
Edited by Jason M. Williamson

I

The Nod

He grasped at the proverbial brass ring of mental freedom only to have his fingertips scrape its surface. "Well," he surmised "I guess another day riding the white horse of my desirable illusion can't hurt." He mumbled to himself, "Hey Mr. DJ, play me another tune while I dance with this devil one more time" Reaching into his pocket to retrieve a neatly folded Dollar bill. Unwrapping it ever so gently to expose a sparkly white powder. a slight grin smeared slowly across his face.

He just cannot seem to shake her loose. His eyes are wide, his nose is raw, and the merry go round does its thang.

Saved by John da' Pope
By Robert Thurston Hankins Jr.

* * *

THE NOD

From behind half-closed, glazed, and bloodshot eyes, John began to regain consciousness as he sat in a lethargic lullaby of waves washing over his body. There in a vacant post office parking lot situated between telegraph and Shattuck Ave. on 48th street he was engrossed in the all too familiar and delightful struggle of fighting a heroin nod. John was a junkie, and he made no qualms about it. He scratches his neck while wafting in and out of cognizance. The sound of the FM radio blaring "you're still a young man, baaabay!" mixed in with the mechanical jungle-like sounds of the neighborhood. Tower of Power crooned across the airwaves caressing and massaging the canal that led to his eardrums. he was able to open one eye to see the local kid Raheem making his way home from school as he did every afternoon at about this time. John slowly looked left at his partners in crime. Del and "Spooky-man" as they leaned and jerked themselves awake repeatedly. John laughed. He was reminded of how "Spooky-man" got his name. he had these large round green eyes that were in stark contrast to his blueish Black skin tone. And to top it off he had light brown hair. Dude was a trip to look at, thought John as he slowly drifted back into the dark cave of his own mind. A few moments slipped by as John continued to scratch the side of his neck until it slightly burned. He leaned closer and closer to the ground until almost falling off the white paint bucket, he had converted into a seat.

Catching himself, John quickly thought "dam, I need to get on home." It was a long trek back to 56[th street] and MLK Blvd. from the vacant post office lot. He slowly struggles to his feet. the euphoric waves of heroin-induced convulsions buckle his knees ever so gently.

John cracked a large grin once he was able to stand straight up "tah-daaaah" he exclaimed to his two friends with a slight giggle, but they were oblivious to his triumph. John mumbled a string of words glued together as his attempt at a farewell to his junkie friends. He received a loud fart and mumbles in return. John began to stumble up Shattuck towards 56th street passing big John's Barbershop and Vern's Market. His feet felt like they were sinking into the concrete which made every step a challenge. Creeping up the street stopping every ten steps to rest and scratch. He took twenty minutes to make it 4 blocks to 51st where an "am pm" gas station stood. John made a left down 51st to cross over to MLK Blvd. he made it to the corner of 51st and MLK just as a police officer was pulling up to the light. John noticed the officer staring in his direction. John was deathly afraid of the Police, OPD was known for beating up black people for no reason and John was not trying to be a victim. John straightened up the best he could, but the weight of his high was like a fifty-pound sandbag on his shoulders. This made him bobble like an apple in a barrel. The Officer just stared in disgust until the light turned green and they went screeching off across the intersection. John took a deep breath thanking God that the encounter did not evolve into an ass-whooping.' at the same time he was disappointed that his high had been blown a bit. The light turned and the white character on the traffic light instructed John to walk. John now with his faculties more in control floated across the street as smooth as a plastic bottle sailing across the ocean on a clear sunny day. John made his way up MLK Blvd. finally reaching his street and then his front door 832 56th a brown duplex house where he and his mother lived after moving from 48th street. Opening the front door, he dragged himself through the Livingroom towards the short hallway passed the family photos and an old black and gold couch, he paused to glance at a picture, it was a photo of his father dressed in his Marine uniform. That picture always sends a jolt of pain to his heart. He really missed him. He floated on lightly with a heavy heart to the doorway that connected the kitchen and a short hall that led to two bedrooms on each end of it. The bathroom was situated in the middle, and John's room was to the left. his mother's room to the right. John opened his door and slipped in closing it behind him. Leaning on the door for a moment, he then stumbled to the four stacked mattresses placed in the corner of his room. Plopping down he stared over at the weight bench. John thought "dam I ain't used that shit in months" before drifting off into a light sleep.

A couple of hours had passed with John sleeping, involuntarily waken slightly every so often. This was an effect of the heroin that he snorted earlier it seemed to never let him fully sleep even though he was sent into deep blissful nods. He could hear someone in the kitchen shuffling pots. He hoped it was his mom getting ready to fix a good meal. He was starving and needed a full home-cooked meal. He stared at the ceiling; his nose focused on a stench that interrupted his gaze. "Dam," John thought "is that me, I smell terrible." John sat up in the bed propping himself up against the wall. He stares in the mirror only seeing his head and shoulders. He looked at his sunken eyes and pale-dry brown skin, a storm of embarrassment showered down on his mind. He cringes at the sight of his own failure in life thus far.

Memories of his life down south in Gaston Alabama wrestled with the Helplessness of his appearance He worked up a grin. "Home," he thought. A stream of memory engulfed his vision. He remembered his life in the hot and humid sun-drenched days of yesterdays long passed. John's' childhood was full of love and wonderment. he would spend his days following his father around the city while he made his collections for the local numbers man. His father an ex-marine who found it hard to get work after his stint in the military had gotten into the numbers racket. His then long-time girl-friend introduced him to her little brother Eddie "Pooh Bear" Jones, a feared man in Gaston. Eddie ran with a crew of well-dressed Gangsters, Eugene, Bob, and Robert T. they called themselves "the four horsemen" and these men were known to shoot first and ask questions later. They ran Gaston's Black community's underworld. John's father worked for them, and this gave John's father a level of prestige and influence. John and his dad were welcomed everywhere. As a child, John would enjoy listening to the adventurous tales of his dad and the Four Horsemen. John wanted to be just like his father.

One day while waiting and listening to music in his father's two-tone white and burgundy 1968 ford falcon John noticed that the picked up was taking a bit longer than usual. John thought about getting out of the car but decided not to, his instructions had always been to never leave the car no matter what. Just then the front door of the store burst open with the owner of the store flying through it and smashing to the ground, glass sloshing everywhere. John was startled. up until now, all the pick-ups had been smooth, in and out. This time he watches as his dad slowly crept into the light. The sound of crushing glass popped under his feet as his smooth panther-like steps brought him closer to the whimpering store owner who was laid out on the sidewalk like a wounded gazelle waiting for the death strike. John's father adjusts his pant legs, to be able to comfortably crouch down beside the man. As he leaned in and said, "you got seventy-two hours Nigga, do you understand me?" the store owner answered between gasped of air and the blood that had filled his mouth from the tooth he lost when hitting the concrete sidewalk. "Yes!" "Yes What!?" yelled John's father yelled. "Yes, Mungu!" the store owner replied. Everyone around was frozen in fear at the sight, including John. Then they heard sirens from far off "it's time to split, baby boy" John's pops shouted to him as he strutted quickly toward the driver's side of the Falcon. Hopping in the front seat swiftly turning the ignition. the expression on his face was oddly jovial in contrast to the situation. John was petrified but his father seemed to glow from the excitement of the prospect of a dangerous run-in with the Cops. "Hey boy! Reach in that glove box and pass me my thang" John's father gleefully instructed. John quickly unlocked the glove box and opened it. his eyes grew large at the sight of a shiny three fifty-seven magnum pistol. John was shocked by what he saw. he was again stuck. His father shouted while pressing the gas pedal "what ya waitin' on boy, pass me the Hamma" John shook out of it and reached in the glove box grabbing the massive death tool and pulled it out slowly. his father quickly snatched it out of his hand. His father grinned; his eyes lit with the elated hysteria of a psychopath who had been huffing laughing gas. "yee haw, mutha fuckas" he yelled. at that moment John felt that he was in a movie he and his father were outlaws on the run from the sheriff. John screamed "woo hoo, go dad" the Falcon was moving at high speeds through the streets. once they made it to the highway John's father pressed the gas pedal to the floor and the engine roared like a lion on the Serengeti, as they flew into the sunset.

Dinner time, the clinging of forks and plates, and the occasional polite instruction to pass a desired portion of the meal were the only sounds heard. John sat at the table with a mouth full of rice. He glanced over at his father who ate with his elbows on the table hovering over his food as if it were going to run away if he did not. John placed his elbows on the table trying to emulate his father. As fast as his elbows hit the table his mother sounds off "uh uh, git cho elbows off my table." John quickly removes them, replying "how come daddy get to put his elbows on the table?" everybody stopped in their tracks. John's' mother's forehead began to wrinkle like a snarling Pitbull. But before she could unleash her bark. John's father spoke up. He said, "Cool it, momma, let me explain it to our smart mouth child" he continued "See, son in this house I'm the king, and your mother is the Queen." John was fully focused on his father's words. "So that makes you are a prince." He followed up with "Our duty is to raise you in the proper manner, so when you are the king of your own house you can do exactly the opposite of, what we instructed you to do" John's father let out a hardy laugh while repeatedly slapping the table. John joins in on the laughter. John's mother became more agitated at Mungu's off humor.

She through a biscuit right at John's father's head and said, "that's why he doesn't listen to me now" John and his father both paused and then laughed even louder. John's mother began to smile. she loved her little family.

suddenly there was a knock at the door. John's father looked over at his wife. Grabbing his handkerchief, he wiped his mouth ridding it of any crumbs from the biscuit that had been hurled at him. He stood up slowly telling his wife that he would get the door. He walked towards the hallway passed the coat rack stopping to retrieve his 357, before proceeding to the door "who is it?" Mungu asked in a firm tone. "It's Robert T." a deep voice shouted back. "Open da dam door man, it urrrrgent" the voice said. Mungu shaking his head in relief shouted back "okay, hold on" as he turned to place his gun back in his coat. He opened the door and in walked Robert T. a six-foot-three brown skin black man who was known for his sharp wit and bodybuilder physique and the way he would draw out his words when he spoke. He always had a joke to tell and everyone who met Robert T. would never forget him. However, this time Robert T. was not bringing jokes. He had some news for Mungu. After the usual handshakes and greetings, Robert T. told John's father that the pickup from earlier was a bad deal. He said, "man you really fucked up, brothaaaa!" he paused, then said. "You know the old man you tossed around todaaay?" John's father replied, "Yeah, what about him?" Robert T. shake his head and whispered as to not let John and his mother hear the news. "shiiiiit, the old dude's heart couldn't take the bangiiiin' against the sidewalk like that, brothaaaaa" he continued "he died right as the pigs pulled up" there was a long silence. Robert T. then went on to say "say brotha, there was a witness who spoke yo naammme, yes suh, suh yes" He then said "you gotta git on, up outta here brothaaaa" Robert T. then reached in his pocket and pulled a hefty sum of cash wrapped in a paper bag. He said, "this is from the horsemen, it's about twenty-thousand dollars ya' diiig?" John's father stood there; stone-faced. He was shocked at the news. His intent was not to kill the old man, but just to scare him into paying his debt. John's father paced back and forth rubbing his head. He was trying to plan his next move. He pounded his fist into the palm of his hand. Shit! He shouted frustrated in the moment. He turned to Robert T. and said "thanks man and tell the brothers I am sorry this happened. I'll repay the bread as soon as I get situated" Robert T quickly responded, "No Suh, keep the bread babeeee" grinning wide he said, "that is on us, baby bubbaaa" John's father thanked him again as Robert T made his way to the door. As he opened the door to leave Robert T. turned back and said, "a word of advice my man," he said, "Never wipe ya ass sideways" he paused looking at the confused look on Mungu's face, and then said, "I mean you can, but you best believe it's gonna be messy." he continued "See you on the battlefield little John" Then Robert T tipped his hat, winked and was gone.

From then on life became a blur for John, he could only remember his parents packing frantically and rushing to the car. He could remember sitting on his knees and looking out the back window of his dad's car as their home became smaller in the distance. They traveled for days only stopping to grab a quick bite to eat at whatever fast food spot that was by the gas stations they refueled at. John's mother asked, "so where are we headed?"

John's father looked at his wife with pride in his eyes and said, "we're going back to my hometown." John smiled and then asked his father "where is that?" his father's smile widened then he answered with utter repletion "shiiiid, Oakland California baby!" his eyes set afire with excitement. this made John wonder why he had never mentioned this place before. The way he went on about how great of a town it was, John felt like he could not wait to get there.

☀ ☀ ☀

II

◎◈◈◈◎

Chapter 2

EVERYBODY GOT CHOICES

It seemed like the days blended on the road. John was stretched out in the back seat with a pillow and cover, relatively comfortable but even then, John was beginning to feel like he was a caged puppy trapped in a kennel. John watched the sunrise and fall 3 times between spells of consciousness and deep sleep.

Finally, the sun rose on the city of Oakland ca. John's father reached back to nudge him. "Hey boy, check this out!" John's father exclaims gleefully as John peers over the car's back door panel out the window he was hit with a barrage of magnificent colors and clothing. All shade of people busy moving around the streets as the car slowly came to a stop at a light John rolled his window down. He overheard two people talking their words sounded funny and they seemed to dance while talking. Hand gestures and loud laughter coalesced into a rhythm. John's' father over the men as well. he grinned in recognition of that scene and sound. He was back.

"Yeah, home sweet home" he yelled. Honking the car horn in a celebratory manner. The warm breeze hitting John's face as he leaned back in the seat, gave him a feeling of euphoria. John notices slight hints of Barbeque in the air John thought it must be where they make it because the smell seemed to be ongoing. Amidst the long cascade of Cadillacs, afros and miniskirts were two men arguing about which one was of more importance. "You must ain't got no job, sucka" one shouted. to which the other replied, "I work for the city!" "Bullshit, you ain't no job sucka." The first man shouted back, and continued "if you really had a job, you'd respect another working man...you... aint... got... no job!" the second man said while making a gesture with his middle finger and then turned to continue sweeping up the dust on the sidewalk. John's mother giggled at the exchange she turns to Mungu and says, "so Mr. man where is our new home?" Mungu replied as he made a turn on 56th street he said, "well now if you look to your right, you shall see it." John's father's voice echoed into the void.

Boom, Boom, Boom John jumped up from his trip down memory lane to the sound of his mother pounding on his door. He answered "what?" the voice on the side sweetly inquired "do you want some dinner?" John sat confused "dinner?" it was just noon. "Dam it, I must have dozed off. he thought to himself. he yelled "yeah, what you fix?" slowly rising to his feet and stretching out his limbs, letting out a long gassy fart. He began to hurry up and get out of his room he knew, one thing for sure a dope fiends' gas is deadly. even though it was his, he could not take the funky stench. Rushing out the door passed his mother as she grabbed her nose to shield her senses from the onslaught of funk that blasted out of John's room, he quickly slid into the bathroom, slamming the door shut behind him. He laughed at his mother's reaction to the foulness that was attacking her nostrils. After taking a much-needed shower John got dressed and went to the kitchen to grab his meal. John's stomach was a tad bit queasy his thoughts jumped quickly to the small balloon he had stashed in his closet the night before. "Oh yeah!" He mumbled to himself as he scooped up a glob of mashed potatoes and slam it on his plate. "A maw!" he yelled "did you eat already?" he asks his mother hoping she had eaten her fill so that he could devour the rest of the chicken she had fried. He replies feel John with joy "Yeah go ahead and eat the rest if you want to" John began to dance around the kitchen spinning and humping in the air while picking up the pieces of chicken left on the grease-soaked napkin on top of the stove.

John thought of eating in the kitchen but opted to go into the living where his mother was. Still dancing with his plate and cup of Kool-Aid he took from the fridge then he boogalooed to the couch and plopped down. His mother shook her head, she was entertained by the display. she was glad her son loved her cooking, as much as she did. However, John's enthusiasm was more for the desert he had hidden from himself in his closet. John would not have to leave the house and could enjoy a night of nodding in and out of consciousness in solitude. John shoveled a heap of mashed potatoes into his mouth "ummmm um, momma these potatoes are smackin'" he managed to say with his jaws full of food. He continued "where you get these from Idaho?" his mother laughed before answering his question. "Shut up, fool." She was reminded of Mungu's humor. John was a chip off the old block. She thought. John blazed through the meal and drank the last bit of cherry red Kool-Aid in his cup hopping up he started towards the kitchen and paused staring at the tv he realized he was so busy eating that he did not even see that his favorite T.V. show the Jefferson's was on. He really loved to see the star George called his neighbor a honky, it really cracked John up. In fact, that became one of John's favorite words when he was upset with any white person, he came across either friend or stranger, they would be a honkey. John continued to the kitchen dropped off his plate and made a beeline straight to his room and closet. He found his stash he opened it set it on his dresser top then walked over to his beatbox, this radio had been a gift his dad had given him before he died, and John made sure to keep it in decent shape. it was cleaned every other day inside and out the plastic chrome nobs had to be sparkling or John did not feel right. After dusting it off a bit John put in the old school tape that his big cousin Jamal had giving him. it was the rap group called the 'Jonzun crew' and the song John always played when he was getting high was a song called "space cowboy" John queued up the tape, turn on his disco light machine he had stolen from a friend's house and prepared for lift-off. For some odd reason, John liked to comb his hair and make his room as neat as possible. it was a strange ritual, but all junkies had one. This was John's. He combed his hair slowly patting down his shag hairstyle. Then he turned and leaned stretching his arm out reaching for the play button, a loud click and suddenly the room was filled with a smooth voice that shouted echoing the word "space cowboy, boy boy" then the beat dropped the kick drum and hand clap reverberating around the cement walls of John room along with the reflection of the lights bouncing from every angled created an ultra-chill atmosphere John took the balloon and gently tore the top of at the knot hold the content in place as to not let the powder spill. Snap! The balloon broke and John turned the balloon over and with his finger and thumb twisted the contents of the balloon onto a dollar that had been folded down the middle so that a crease ran from one end to the other once the heroin was emptied into the dollar it was folded neatly John took his lighter and laid it flat on top of the dollar to and began to rub it over it back and forth until the dope was flat this was done to make sure there were no lumps that would fall out of John's nose when he snorted the brown dust. John grabbed his stash. while holding it he watched its crystals flicker in the red, green, and blue disco lights "space cowboy, boy, boy. now echoed off John's eardrums adding to is his excitement, continuing to set the mood. his eyes grew watery as he prepared for the initial burn in his nostril followed by the sweet drain. John reached into his dresser drawer, fumbled through the clothes folded inside it, and pulled out a teeny tiny spoon that had been made especially for these occasions; he gingerly dipped the tiny spoon into the dollar's belly as if he was trying to tickle a fairy. the lyrics from the song blared "he's bad, he's mean, he's the space cowboy with his laser beams" as John lifted the brown dust to his nose "he's bad, he's number one, he's the space cowboy with a laser gun" the M.C.'s words pounded against John's mind as he exhaled through his mouth and then sniffed the dope violently up high into his right nostril instantly a single tear sparkled from the corner of his right eye and rolled down his cheek. As he Blasted off, cowboy John was now riding into the ethers.

☀ ☀ ☀

III

Chapter 3

THE DEVIL IS DOPE

6 am, John's alarm broke the silence of the morning. John slowly opened his eyes trying to gain some clarity. he reached for his phone as it vibrated and screamed. John startled at the position he was in; he had managed to nod off in the corner of his room naked, except for the one raider sock. the silver and blacks pirate staring him in his face with a look of judgment. John looked around and rose to his feet he grabbed his pants from the day before. they had been thrown over his dresser mirror. He then grabbed his shirt sniffing the armpit to see if it could be worn again without offending anyone who had gotten too close to him. One quick sniff with no effect because his nostrils that had been stuffed with heroin the night before did little to detect any stench from the dingy shirt. He put it on and along with his other raider sock, shoes, and headed for the door. John was on his way to trying and cop a fix of that brown "Booger Sugar" as he and his friend referred to it. In a flash John was on the

streets headed to "spooky-mans" house this was where he had headed for the last two years of his junkie career. He lived in the "Roach Ville" apartment complex about a 20-minute walk from John's house. It was a clear blue sky on a midwinter's day in Oakland which meant cold but sunny, this is typical weather in the bay area. as John hurried through the streets, he saw a group of older guys who he recognized as Chuck and his cousins Kenny, Von, and Larry they were the neighborhood hustlers who protected the younger people in the area. chuck was known for his karate skills; it was rumored that he was a 5th-degree black belt. He always wore his karate uniform everywhere he went. As John passed the group, he greeted the group with a nod to which the group returned acknowledging head nods well everyone except chuck who slapped his hand into his fist and bowed. John stopped and bowed back, half out of respect and the other half for not wanting chuck to kick his ass. John proceeded on his mission his stomach was starting to feel funny, and the gas had already begun to escape from his ass. every few steps a pop of smelly air would leap out of him. He quickened his steps passing gas the whole way. Finally reaching Roach Ville apt. he ran to the back to where apt number 3 was and knocked on the door. Five seconds later it opened and a cloud of marijuana smoke exploded into the hallway. "What up my brotha?" a half-black, half Pilipino man greeted John. He replied quickly "yo Will, what's the word?" "ain't nothing I can't fix" will urbanely replied with a slick grin on his face. He knew why John had come. He turned and headed to a room located at the end of a long hallway. He opened the door to reveal spooky-man bagging up a small mountain of heroin from a large silver tray. Looking up to see who it was coming in spooky-man smiled widely. "My Nigaaah" spooky shouted. Will shut the door after letting John through. John plopped down on the bed. he was a bit tired from the walk. He said, "shit spooky, how do you put all that shit in them balloons and not get down?" spooky-man paused for a long while then looked up and mumbled "ain't nothing free, but" bam, bam, bam! he was cut off in mid-sentence by a hard knock at the door. "What is it, Goddam it?" it was Will, he said "hey man Del out here, should I let him in?" spooky grinned showing his two missing teeth on the left side of his mouth "of course, of course, we are open for business" he continued while holding up a balloon plucking it with his finger "and business is good... mutha fucka!" Will laughed and gestured to Del to come to the back room. Once in del slapped five with John and Spooky-man. Then he began to peel off a twenty-dollar bill and tossed it too spooky. John realized the time had come to get high, and instantly shoves his hand into his back pocket for the ten-dollar he had managed to talk his mother out of at dinner the night before. Gave it to spooky-man with an embarrassed smirk on his face hoping spooky would let him slide on the ten he had owed him. Spooky quickly grabbed the ten and placed it on the bed beside him not saying a word. he tossed Del two blue balloons of stuff. He went back to bagging up the rest of the heroin. John was nervous now because he did not want to say anything and have spooky-man flip out on him, but he also wanted his dope. A while went by, Del had prepared his fix and began to snort his portion he passed the folded dollar bill to John feeling sorry for him knowing that he was in a tough spot. John did not take the dollar, instead, he stared at Spooky man to see if there was any anger in his eyes. Spooky-man stared back with his blue eyes and slowly cracked a smile. He then asked, "What Nigga?" to which John replied "dude, I do not get mine?" again spooky man fell out laughing he said "you a cold junkie, nigga; boy I tell ya. He continued, "Look! you shit head." John looked down to a plate beside him, John felt stupid and relieved at the same time. spooky-man had already set up a little something for John and had slid the plate to him, but John was so busy looking at the large mountain of drugs being bagged up he did not even notice. John quickly took his little spoon out of the inside pocket in his coat, a little embarrassed he giggled as he dug into the small hill and took a sharp snort. John felt something was different about this batch of dope in fact it seemed that the dope was somehow different every time, but John shrugged it off and finished his plate. "High is high," he thought to himself.

After getting good and loaded and all the dope had been bagged up it was time to venture into the streets. the guys loved floating around Oakland half-awake on a cloud of heroin-induced Euphoria. Del held the small FM radio that accompanied them everywhere. it was always tuned to their favorite radio station KSOL they only played smooth jazz and r&b this was the soundtrack to the high. They walked slowly to the bus stop on Broadway. there they waited for the 51-bus line to take them downtown. After a ten-minute wait, the bus came screeching up. the bus's engine waking them from their standing nods. They all hopped on, spooky-man paying the fair for the three of them. They floated and stumble to the back of the bus where they could sit and fade away in peace away from the eyes of judgment, slamming their gavel-like stares down upon them condemning them to life in a prison of shame. After twenty minutes of riding the wave of potholes and abrupt stops in traffic, they hit 14th street. del pulled the line to signal to the driver they wanted off. The bus slowed and pulled to the side then stopped. the back door opened, and the fellas jumped off in the heart of the city. Del turns up the groove on the radio. Kool and the gangs 'Summer Madness' blares from the speakers as all three stopped in their tracks, "aww shit!" John says with a long-drawn-out slurring voice. the heroin was causing his jaws to flop around his face like a beach ball being slapped from side to side. The three happy junkies danced their way up fourteenth street headed for Lake Merritt. This was a body of water that sat right in the middle of the city it separated north and west Oakland from the east side. It was neutral territory and everybody from Oakland came there to kick back listen to music and eat decent food from the local vendors and restaurants that lined the streets. After a ten-minute strut, the brother made it to a prime location. A large tree on the east side of the lake they all copped a piece of ground. laying here they could watch the scantily dressed girls as they strolled past. Spooky-man had pulled a bottle of thunderbird from his back pocket and placed it between his legs to hold it from falling over as he poured the cherry-flavored Kool-Aid he had retrieved from his coat. "Yes, yes, yes!" he said half-singing his words. "Gentlemen, I say welcome to the good life. Jack!" "Sho-Nuff!" John shouted back while reaching over to slap Del five. A loud pop exploded from their hand's collision. "Hey baby pass the Liqueurs" del said in his hip cat British voice. To which Spooky man obliged "yes sah" they passed around the bottle a few times. They were still high from the heroin they had earlier, and the wine and Kool-Aid made it even better to them so much so that they did not see the police car slowly roll up to their right. The two-office sat there for a while and observed the three giggling and singing between nods. the officers got out of the car one of them slammed his door to alert the three of their presents. "Aww shit man it's the rollers" John whispered out the corner of his mouth. "mutha fuck a duck" Del mumbled. At that moment spooky man leaped to his feet and started to run. One of the officers pulled his gun and pointed it at Del and John and screamed "don't move your black asses a millimeter or I'll put a bullet in you junkie asses" "put your goddam hands!" the other cop gave chase. John could see that even though spooky-man was high as hell he was a lot faster than the cop that was falling further behind until he gave up running. Del grinned as spooky-man kept running. But the cop was not given up the capture of his suspect. The cop went to one knee and yelled "Gun! I see a gun" and then the cop aimed his pistol and let off six quick shots all but one hitting spooky-man in the leg, Back, and Head. Red Flesh and skull hurled into the air as Spooky man took a few more strides his lifeless body fell in the intersection. a river of blood streamed from the openings in his body turning his clothes crimson. John and del lay there in shock, not a word were they able to mutter. John could feel his heart pounding against his chest as a wave of tears flushed into his eyes. He shook his head to try to gain some type of clarity he thought "the sight he just witnessed, couldn't have been real" he turned towards Del who had urinated on himself from the mixture of fear, and the carnage he just saw. Del took a long deep breath and with his eyes bulging from his face; his mouth ajar showing his inner throat, screamed with agony the pain reverberating through the earth and John's soul. John could only bury his face in the dirt and let his tears water the soil. More police cars arrived on the scene as a crowd began to gather. Del and John were both hurried into separate police cars, where they stayed for the next two hours. Every ten minutes or so an office would open the door to ask some dumb question like "do you guys live in the area?" or "what type of drugs were you using?" but John could not speak he would just shrug his shoulders. And stare out the cage-covered window. John could feel the cold steel of the handcuffs that is cutting into his skin even if moved in the slightest bit. His attention was held by a flash of a slave. he imagined being held in the bowels of a Slave ship with these types of handcuffs on his wrist for three months sometimes even longer. He wanted to be free. Free from the moment, free from the junkie's life, and free from people who would kill a kid because he had embarrassed him by simply being able to run faster. John looked up to the roof of the police car and whisper with the weight of his turmoil on his heart. he said "please God. please take me away from this place, I do not want this no more. Please, please, please!" Then John took a deep breath, and all at once, John was startled by a knock on the police cars' window. John jerked his head expecting to see another officer about to ask him more stupid questions, but to his surprise, it was an old black man. His clothes were dusty and covered in stains. His eyes were bloodshot red and his teeth yellow, but the bottom row was gold and still sparkled in the setting sun's rays. He said, "hey brotha-man, you want freedom?" John turned his head to ignore the crazy person. John looked down shaking his head and turned to his left to look out the other window, but the man's face was already there, but this time more stern and menacing. John jumped back from the window. "Get the fuck outta here man" the old man cracked a yellow tooth smile and said, "if you want freedom, you gone have to pay" John yelled, "leave me alone mutha fucka!" "You are alone" the old man replied. "you're on a slave vessel, baby" he continued "one you can't get off without my help." John was momentarily frozen by what the man was saying. he thought, how he knew he was just thinking about being on a slave ship? Just then the old man laughed and spun around "surprise nigga!" the old man backed away from the police car as a police officer was walking up. John watched as the old man bumped into the officer. the officer yelled "watch where you're going, you bum" the old man just bowed his head, humped the air, and tiptoed away. But before leaving he turned to look over his shoulder and yelled "God is all there is" he then stumbled off into the sunset. The police officer opened the door and began pulling John out of the car the officer went through his pockets checking for any weapons or drugs. John explained to the office that he had been thoroughly patted down twice before; he did not have anything on him. the officer told John you're involved in a shooting your friend had a gun, and we want to make sure you and the other friend you got left are clean. John replied, "spooky didn't have a gun and that pig shot him in the back!" suddenly the cop turned John around and pressed him against the car by his collar to the point John began to gasp for air. He stared John deep in his eyes and said "listen you black piece of shit, accidents happen all the time and I'd hate to see one happen to you right now" at this time John was starting to pass out from the tight grip. The cop's chokehold was released when a bottle splashed across the hood of his car. It was some young kids from West Oakland. John could tell because one of them had on a 32nc and Linden shirt. more bottles began to whistle through the air braking all around all the officers and their cars. John was quickly shoved back into the car. the officer hopped in the front seat and took off heading down to the station. John now found himself in an interrogation room. His stomach in knots his muscles aching from the need for a fix. it had now been ten hours since his last snort of heroin and the junkie sickness was on him, bad. John was dripping with sweat by the time a large white man opened the door to the small, all-grey-green room. A dim yellowish light in the center of the ceiling made the corners of the tiny box slightly shaded John could barely see the faces of the other men who follow behind the big white cop. As they lined the walls the head cop grabbed a wooden chair and spun it around to sit with the back of the chair toward John. John recalled seeing this movie on all the cop shows he had watched with his mother. "Dam! My mother" John thought realizing the shooting was all over the news by now and that she was having a fit. The big white cop snapped his finger to get John's attention. He said, "what up homeboy, what turf you claim?" "you one of the Bushrod high cats?" "or" he went on "maybe you from Down by Gaskill? You do not look like you from the west and you dam sure ain't from the Deep East." John paused for a few seconds and answer in a low tone "I'm from the north that's it just the north." The big white man said, "look my name is Detective Buttinsky, De...Tec...Tive, do you understand what that means punk!" John shook his head up and down and said "yeah." Buttinsky replied "good, so you know, that I know, that you know what the fuck I mean when I ask you WHERE THE FUCK YOU FROM!?" John again nodded saying "yeah." "Great!" buttinsky shot back. "Now listen up shit head I ain't got no time to play with no junky nigger. you are not in trouble here. I do not think, we found anything on you." The detective said while grinning in a sly fashion. John sat straight up in his chair and tilt his head slightly to the left and asked confused "you don't think" buttinsky stood up whipping his chair around and sat back down reclining. he crossed his legs left over right and said in a nonchalant manner "yeah, Johnny maybe we found something on you and maybe we didn't, and it all depends on if your buddy had something on him and I'm sure you know he had a gun, right Johnny?" John paused for a long while. his mind racing from one decision to the other spooky man was dead. So, it would not matter much to say he did have a gun. John pondered and the tic toc from the clock that sat high on the wall over the exit door grew louder... Then John thought about spooky's family and how they would not have any justice if he lied. The urge to defecate made John's decisions even harder to make clear in his mind. Finally, John said, "shit you pigs always pulling some bullshit like this out cha ass, but this time it ain't finna work jack!" John continued "it was not just me out there who saw that pig murder my friend and I ain't fixing to back down and lie like a bitch for no stankin' ass cop...FUCK YOU!" the detective and the other officers were falling over one another trying to get their pound of flesh.

They kick, punched, and stomped John for fifteen minutes without a single pause. One officer had kicked John in the stomach making defecate all over the floor and they still did not stop the brutal punishment until the bloody stole's stench was too much to take. One cop yelled after lifting John up by the front of his shirt "Goddam, this junkie shit smells like the circus has come to town" right before delivering a deadly right hand to John's left temple knocking him out cold.

☼ ☼ ☼

IV

Chapter 4

CHILDHOOD TRAUMA

An hour later the loud steady buzz of the dim lite bulb that protruded from the far corner of the otherwise pitch-black cell stuttering its low shine every now and again Seem to be the only way John could determine he was still alive beside the throbbing pain that shot from every cell in his body. John just lay there for fear that if he would move, he would find out just how many bones had been broken in the ass-whipping he took at the hands and feet of those hoe ass cops. John whimpered in the dark, he was so fearful of what life was going to throw at him next, that he just laid there thinking, staring at the light bulb thinking about dying. he asked aloud to the light bulb "is this how I die?" John began to cry louder as the pain of his wounds shot through every limb, he could barely open his swollen eyes as the blood dripped from their gashes. He begged the light bulb to "please let me die" John whimpered "please I cannot take it anymore!" his fear grew as he was realizing that he would soon be visited by the dreaded sickness he so desperately tried to stay ahead of by shoving heroin into his nostrils daily. He wanted to go home, not the physical home he and his mother shared but the image of home that represented his happiness. The happiness he once knew back before the night his dad had died.

The memory instantly drove the pain from his body towards his heart. When his father was alive life was not entirely heaven, however, it was bliss compared to the lowest levels of hell John had come to know. John sunk into a blurry dream of memories that dulled the sting of loss ever so slightly his eyes glossing over as they peer into the dim light. He remembered the birthdays and Christmas presents that lined the tall green tree that stood as tall as the ceiling and how the trees pine smell filled the small home. He thought about thanksgiving, the food cooked by his aunt "Dimples" who was named that because on the day she was born she smiled, and two deep dimples were prominent on her little round face. John continued to drift down memory lane for a moment in that dark cell. John's' fond recollections subsided. He thought about the dark times as well he thought about the time had been caught playing with matches by his mother. And though John begged his mother not to tell his father she told him and what followed was a beating as brutal as the one he had just taken. Mungu had punished John so severely that John's hand had become injured. John's thumb was not able to move, John explained his injuries to his mother and she, in turn, mentioned the complaint to John's father to which he replied "oh yeah? Well, I bet he will not play with no more matches, I will tell ya that." John continued to stare into the flickering glow of the light bulb in his cell. John asked himself "how could a father do his son like that without remorse?" John's mind quickly transitioned to a rainy day not too long after the beating. His father was sitting in John's room. John remembered how he stared at his father with admiration even after the barbarous slave-like whipping he had given him. John loved his father like a mindless robot incapable of understanding that he should hate him for the abuse he endured. As the raindrops collided with the glass of the window, adding to the grey shaded moment. John's father looks over and asks, "Hey man, you wanna go get a train?" John confused by the offer balled up his forehead, slightly looking upwards, and replied, "heck yeah!" Mungu leaped to his feet turn swiftly to the bedroom door and said cheerfully "well come on, good brotha!" John hopped up and snatching his coat quickly followed his father to the front door. John's father turned to John's mother and smiled widely saying "hey we'll be back." John's' memory cleared for a second, as he lay in the cell. he understood now that his mother's head nod was a signal to John's father and that she was proud of him. John continued to reminisce about that day slowly turning onto his back. falling back into his thoughts. He remembered after getting into the car. John's father turned on the engine to warm it up before putting the vehicle in gear. John's father turned the headlights on and using his palm he turned the steering wheel around to right three times. he released the brake pedal and tapped the gas. the large car leaped and roared into traffic. they headed up Martin Luther King Blvd. on their way to Berkeley, a neighboring city filled with free thinkers and hippies. "I really love Berkeley," John thought as he continued his recall of the memory. John and his dad had reached the hardware store. Mungu parked right in front. they both hopped out and rushed into the store both grinning in anticipation of seeing the trains available inside. John pushed the front door to the store open, a bell clanged as it was struck by the door's metal frame. The store was filled with people. some there to get too s and other equipment to finish housing projects. other like John and his dad were there to purchase a train which at that time was the usual thing at hardware stores around the Bay area. John's' dad began grabbing everything he needed for the train. John was surprised at how much stuff his dad was getting. some of it did not seem to have anything to do with a train at all. John just watched as his dad grabbed wood, screws, fake grass, and finally a box containing an actual train John's' dad placed all the materials on the counter. The older store clerk smiled and said, "oh somebody going to build a town, I see." To which Mungu replied "yes sir, just like Allensworth" the store clerk's face suddenly changed from a large smile to a blank gaze. He replied, "that's nice." Then he hurried to get the items totaled and then bagged up. Mungu grabbed all the big bags and nodded for John to get the smaller ones. it was so many bags John felt like they had bought the whole store. After packing the trunk with all the bags. John and his father hopped back into the car heading home. John and his dad laughed at jokes from Richard Pryor that John's father had on cassette tapes. As they cruise down MLK Blvd. occasionally Mungu would honk his horn at some friends he would recognize on the corners as we passed. One such friend was 'Old Bob Cooch' everybody in the neighborhood called him "coochi-man" he was known for harassing the women as they went in and out of Vern's markets. He sat by the door and proclaimed his affection by saying "hey baby, I sho' likes what I see!" the women would be horrified and that made it even funnier to youngsters who hung around Vern's to watch Bob do his thing.

The car slowed up as John's father pulled into Vern's parking lot. Mungu crept up on where Old Bob was and rolled down his window. Bob got up without saying a word and came to the car Mungu reached down into his coat pocket pulled out a five-dollar bill handed it to bob. Bob grabbed the crisp bill and folded it into his shirt pocket and said, "the world is cold, but your heart is warm, when that changes, here comes the storm." John's father replied, "Right on, Coochiman" "I'll see ya later Brotha" while rolling up his window. He put the car in gear and crept off heading home. they drove for a couple of blocks and then John asked his father "why do you give, coochie-man, money?" Mungu looked over at John and quickly back at the road and explained "we are a people who learn through stories, signs, and symbols." He went on "the way our people transfer information is highly valuable, not only to us but to the entire population of humans around the world." Mungu paused then he said "you see old bob cooch is a griot and he comes from a lengthy line of Mystical storytellers who pass down the wisdom to the rest of us. I pay coochi-man for his service. And in fact, when you get old enough to start making your own money you need to find a griot to help you navigate through life, that's of course if Old Bob Cooch isn't around...you dig me?" John nodded in the affirmative. As the 68' Falcon floated on. By the time we had reached the house, the streetlights had come on and the sun was about gone the grayish clouds turned a darker shade of purple as nightfall became our backdrop. Once parked John's father rushed to get all the bags into the house, it seemed that he was more trying to show his wife what he had done. John's father was seeking some sort of acknowledgment and redemption of some kind. Stumbling in the doorway to reveal his goods like a pirate showing off his newly stolen booty. "Hey baby, come see what we got!" John's father shouted as John himself fumbled with the large bags. he echoed his dads' words "yeah momma come look, my daddy bought the whole store!" Mungu's smile extended even wider as he felt the pride in his son's voice, after all, it was him who he wanted to empress in the first place. John's mother rushed into the front room to her surprise she saw 5 large bags plus 4 smaller bags that John had in his arms. John's mom who stood in the kitchens entranceway leaned to the side folding her arms, and said "wow, that is a lot of stuff." She was satisfied with Mungu's attempt.

Mungu scooped up the bags and rushed to John's room to set up the Train. He first laid out the wood and then he took measurements. He drew lines, marked spots, and drilled holes. He was a craftsman and a master mason. After about two six-packs of Mickey's malt liquor and three hours of drilling, hammering and gluing. Mungu took a step back and admired his design. It was a well-crafted 4ft high table. on top of it lay a small replica of a country town. John's' dad turned to him and said "there's only one thing missing" then John's dad took out a small signboard and gave it to John. He said, "here son, you have to give your town a name" John took the small board and paintbrush and went to the kitchen table to think of a name. it did not take John long to think of the perfect name for the town John wrote on the sign "Welcome to Allensworth" he had heard his dad mention Allensworth at the store, and he had heard bob cooch tell stories about how a former slave named Allen Allensworth escaped his bondage and became a Union soldier and the very first African American lieutenant colonel.

afterward, he became a preacher and a teacher, but according to coochie-man, his greatest achievement was building the first town financed and governed by African Americans in California. John finished the sign and handed it to his father. Mungu grabbed the sign, holding it up for a long while just staring at it. At that moment John realized there was more to the building of this train and replica town. This was Mungu's way of apologizing for the harsh treatment of his son. Mungu realized that it was out of the fear of losing his son and wife from an accident that made him react like that. Mungu also understood that he could not ever do that again and that he had to be more calculating in his decision-making. He had to *keep his heart warm in this cold world*" John's father looked down at him and said, "let's always build and never destroy, and if we must destroy, let it only be to build something better in its stead" John nodded understanding the statement. Then John's dad placed the sign at the town's entrance.

This was the last time John and Mungu would do anything together. the very next night tragedy struck. While John was washing dishes, he overheard a commotion from the neighbor's house. This was not a new thing since the neighbors always threw loud parties, that constantly got out of hand. Fights occurred frequently and the police were there to take control of whatever situation had taken place. But this time

John heard his father's voice within the melee. He was going back and forth hurling insults with someone whose voice John did not recognize. John turned the water from the sink off to hear better. They were cursing and John could hear different voices trying to calm John's dad down but to no success. John turned toward the Livingroom and yelled to his mother to come to listen. John's mother who was enjoying her favorite tv show let out a sigh and reluctantly got up and went to the kitchen window. When she listened closely, she heard John's father. She turned and told John to go to his room. She grabs her coat from her room and then walked to the front door saying "I'm going to get your dad; I'll be right back" she rushed out the door slamming it behind her. John rushed back to the kitchen window where he could hear his mother pleading with Mungu to leave and come home. Once John's mother had entered the neighbor's home, she found out the argument between Mungu and the man whose name was "Tee" was over a woman who had been secretly seeing Mungu for a few months she had just shown up at the party and Mungu was upset with her and Tee tried to step in. that was disrespect in Mungu's eyes, and this cause the rift between the Two Men. John's mother hearing this began to scream and hit Mungu who while trying to deflect her punches knocks her to the ground. At this point, Tee jumps up and pushes Mungu back saying "hey man you've lost your mind!" without thinking Mungu drove a vicious left hook to Tee's jaw knocking him to the ground. The crowd managed to grab Mungu long enough for Tee to get up and stumble out of the house. Mungu slipped out of the hands of the crowd and went after Tee. By this time John's mother had risen to her feet and made her way outside. she ran back to the house where John was, she grabbed him, and his coat pleading with him to hurry and put on his shoes. John had only one of his shoes on when his mother snatched him up and out the front door. Headed down the stairs, John could see a trail of blood leading to an open car door. On the other side of the car was Tee with a busted lip grasping a small gun and Mungu on the other side holding a pocketknife.

As John and his mother scurried past the two men locked in a standoff. Tee tried to run but quickly realize this was a mistake he was not going to outrun Mungu. As John and his mother turned the corner, John looked back to see his father and Tee fall behind a car across the street. As soon as he and his mother were out of sight, they heard two loud pops. John let go of his mother's hand and ran as fast as he could only hearing his mother's voice screaming for him to keep running.

January 30[th]1975 at 10:35 pm Mungu was dead.

John awoke from his daydream of a time long passed. it had been fifteen years since his father had been killed and since then his life had been turned upside down. After Mungu's death, John struggled with what it meant to be dead. And it was not until he began to realize that Mungu's absence was permanent did he start to look at his own life from a slightly blurred field.

The pain of his father's death was too much for his young mind to bear and so a buffer like consciousness developed in his personality. as if his brain was trying to protect itself from the sudden jabs of sadness that would stab his whole body at the simple memory of Mungu. John had developed a Mental illness but no one around him could see it. His mother just thought it was him being a little eccentric and nothing more. But John's ability to focus on school was all but nonexistent. John would often "space out" in the classroom and while in conversations with people. John would just stare with a blank look. some people would catch it and ask if he was okay, to which John would just say "yeah, I'm just daydreaming." John knew something was wrong, but he could not explain it to anyone.

. John had managed to prop himself up on the cement slab in the back of the cell next to the shit-stained toilet that was supposed to be a bed but was more like a medieval torture device. It had a very thin cold plastic mattress on top of the slab that give no comfort to anybody who laid on it. It smelled like someone had relieved themselves on it a couple of hundred times, the stench was nauseating. John had no choice but to lay on it. when he sat up his ribs screamed out to his brain with jolts of fiery pain. John laid on his back with one hand under his head like a pillow and continued to think about his past. John attended Claremont middle school which was located on the border between Berkeley and Oakland on Claremont Avenue on the Oakland side. Middle school was a conundrum for John he never got used to the different classes in one day schedule. It did not make sense that every hour and fifteen minutes he had to go to another class with another teacher with a different attitude and set of rules that he would have to learn.

John did not do well in important classes like Math, English, and Science. But he did excel in art and P E. the latter being easy for him because he had been playing on the local pop warner football team called the Oakland Dynamites.

John loved drawing and was quite good at it. He was able to draw anything and make it look realistic by incorporating the smallest details. That is how John would spend most of his classes doodling different characters and creating stories to match the picture. *Kinda like the one you are reading now.* John's school days were filled with daydreams, drawing, and fights, lots of fights. One fight, John recalled while in the darkness of his cell was with a bully by the name of Oliver.

On this day Oliver would find out why it was not good to mess with the quiet kid. One day while playing touch football in the yard, Oliver thought it would be funny to trip John when he had gotten the ball. John's team needed a touchdown before the bell rang. and they all knew that John was the fastest on the squad so everybody including the opposite team knew the ball would end up in John's hands. the two teams lined up in the hot sun. its rays beaming down on the sweaty faces of the tiny black gladiators as they prepared for one last play.

This was life and death, the agony of defeat or the joy of triumph. The quarterback surveyed the field, and then. Set, hut, hut growled the quarterback, hike!!! He commanded his troops into action. The front lines collided with one another as the defense tried to stop the play before it developed. but it was a sweep to the right. the whole offense moved towards the right side of the makeshift football field as the quarterback faked a "keeper." As the defense closed in on the quarterback, he slickly tosses the ball to John. The defense screams out "get John!" but John was too agile, and he leapt and cut in the opposite direction slicing through the defensive line like a grizzly bear's tooth through salmon flesh. Like a young Barry

Sanders, John shook and juked his way to open field and began to rush for the endzone. John was running full speed; he did not notice Oliver on the sideline. His face, equipped with a devious grin. As he waited til John got closer. John made the mistake of looking back at his pursuers and that gave Oliver enough time to move into position and stick his foot out, catching John's foot in full stride. John's face quickly turned from pride and excitement to horror, as he went flying into the air headfirst. He rose in the air, flailing his arms and legs like a baby bird learning to fly. He must have flown 10 feet before crashing into the ground scraping his chest and chin. The chorus of loud groans from the other players and onlookers was the barometer of the severity of the sight they had just witnessed. "Holy shit," said one boy as he covered his face with his hands. All the other players as well as the other kids on the playground ran over to see if John was still alive.

John just laid there for a minute waiting for the stinging in his chess to subside. Once he was able to get up, he did so with the intention to completely decimate Oliver. John rose quickly and slowly turned towards Oliver. the crowd parted to give John a full view of his victim. John wiped the blood from his chin, looking at it and then showing it to Oliver. John smiled and said, "you've spilled my blood, and now you will have to repay me with your own." A boy in the crowd said, "ooooh shit!" Oliver stood there, confused by the weird display. Then Oliver replied, "dude if you don't get your weird-ass on somewhere, you ain't bout to do shit" the crowd gasped, and then like lighting shot out of a cannon, John pounced on Oliver. John's fist cut Oliver every which way but loose. Rights left and uppercut. Mike Tyson would have been proud. When John finally got tired of whipping on Oliver's ass the yard guards whose job it was to make sure things like this did not happen, could only gasp at the carnage. One guard asked, what happened? as the other two guards pulled John off Oliver. The other kids who had witnessed the whole thing told that Oliver had tripped John and made him scrape his chin and chess. The one guard looked over at Oliver who was barely alive and shook her head and said, "Goddam, I bet he won't trip nobody else...shiiiid!" and all the other kids and even the other two guards on the yard started to laugh. John grinned slightly at the memory.

Just then a short black cop comes to the cell and begins to unlock it. "Mungu, John Mungu!" the cop yelled "get your ass up you have been bailed out. git your shit." Then he waved his hand in front of his face after catching a whiff of John's crap-filled pants, and says "pee-yew, yeah hurry up and get yo shit out of here, literally." While chuckling he exclaimed, "boy you smell like a dead man."

John was too embarrassed to say anything. The cops led him to the processing room where they took a picture and fingerprinted him. usually, this is done when entering the jail, but the detectives had a different agenda last night. John was then led to the front of the station where his mother was waiting for him. she ran up and hugged him tightly they both began to cry. John's mother then said, "Jesus you stink!" John giggled and hugged her a little bit tighter.

    ☀ ☀ ☀

Chapter 5

CLOSE ENCOUNTER OF THE MAGIC KIND

The ride home from the downtown police station was quiet. John's mother had all the windows rolled down to let out some of the funk from John's bowels. It was not such a bad idea since it was a nice evening the crisp air danced whimsically through the falcon's interior like a graceful ballet dancer. John's mother broke the silence with the inquiry "did you cooperate with the detectives?" John still staring out the open window, answer without expression "naw." John did not want to tell his mother he had been beating half to death by the detectives. He figured it would only worry her more and she already worried enough for two lifetimes over the last 24 hours. He would just keep that to himself. Besides, the two swollen eyes should've tipped her off. He figured she did not ask about his eyes, because she did not want to hear the gruesome truth.

They finally reach their home and John gingerly walked to the stairs and up into the house. Making his way straight to his room. John thought about the heroin he stashed at the lake when the cops first pulled up. He tossed it in the bushes nearby. He said he would go back to check to see if it were still there tomorrow. But tonight, he would have to rely on the "Robo" he kept in the freezer for emergencies like this. "Robo" was a prescription that doctors gave to their patients who had severe coughs Robitussin cough medicine and codeine was used frequently by heroin addicts to curb the sickness until they could cop a real fix. John took off the smelly clothing and opted to throw them away. There was no sense in keeping them, they would only remind him of the beating and the death of his friend "spooky-man" who had been a part of John's life since he first got to 56th street. In fact, it was spook who introduced John to drugs and alcohol, and now he was gone and left John to carry this heavy monkey all by himself.

Once John had discarded the cloth funky clothes, he went to the bathroom to run the shower. he examined his wounds in the mirror still not believing he did not buckle under that vicious ass whipping. "I am one tough mutha fucka," he said to himself while bringing his face within an inch of the mirror as the steam from the shower engulfed his view.

Stepping gingerly into the shower, John's cuts stung under the hot water. as John dabbed his face with the warm washcloth tiny streams of blood ran down his body and pooled at his feet, before oozing down into the drain. Grabbing the soap and smashing it between his palms and the clothe John watched the white suds becoming pink as it mixed with his blood. John began to cry once more, but this time not for himself but for his friend. He sobbed deeply for twenty minutes. The warm water cleaning his wounds will never penetrate the injuries to his mind. Finally, John managed to get out of the shower and get dressed, he put on his favorite basketball shorts, which he had gotten from the Cal Berkeley store. A team store located on the Cal Berkeley campus. That is where he, spooky-man and del used to go to get high and watch the white girls go back and forth to class.

After grabbing a white tee shirt John went to the kitchen to retrieve his "Robo" he reached all the way in the back behind all the frozen meats. John kept it there for two reasons, one so his mother would not bother it and two because keeping it frozen made it thick so when he pulled it into a soda or juice, it would not pour too fast. Accidentally pouring too much would be a waste. But as he searched for the "Robo" he quickly realized that it was not where he had left it. He moved a few packages of meat so that he could confirm his fears. "nothing" he thought while beginning to Panic. He called to his mother with a nervous voice full of false nonchalant confidence. "Ma!" John said, "Hey Ma!" he called out again. "What?" his mother's voice blared back from her room. "Hey, did you happen to see a bottle of purple juice, sitting in the back of the freezer?" John squinted his eyes hoping for an answer that led to him finding his "Robo." "That bottle of Kool-Aid?" she replied "yeah" John answered with a hint of hope. Yeah, I gave it to the neighbor's kids right before I came to get you this morning, it had been in the freezer for so long I figure you did not want it." She continued to explain "they were outside in front playing, and I thought they may have been thirty; so, I offer them some grape Kool-Aid." Just then John dropped to his knees, "what the fuck?" he said under his breath, those kids are going to fuckin die if they drink all that Robitussin!" "Holy shit balls" John whispered. Then he hopped to his feet stumbled out the back door and came up the driveway headed for the neighbor's house. John knocked on the door and he heard a voice ask, "who is it?" "It is me, John, from next door!" the voice on the other side answered half talking and have singing "I'll beee right thereee!"

The door opened slowly to reveal a beautiful woman in her late thirties, wearing a robe that barely kept her large breast hidden from John's sight. Her eyes were low, and she seemed a bit aloft in her demeanor. she swayed back and forth slightly as she spoke. She said softly "what can I do for you young man?" her voice sultry and relaxed. John was stuck for a second, then he snapped out of it, remembering why he was there. he said, "Ms. Adesokan, my mom gave your kids some Kool-Aid earlier and I'm afraid it may have been old and not good for them." Then he continued with "as a matter of fact if you still have the bottle, it came in I kind of need that back." Ms. Adesokan stood there for a long moment her eye shut. She then jerked herself awoke and said, "call my Sharon, and o'yeah that Kool-Aid was way too thick, I think it was concentrated so I made a whole pitcher of it, and dam it was good" John's knees buckled when he heard that. He replied, "did you use it all?" Sharon mumbled while nodding out slowly "naw baby, it was so thick I just use half the bottle" she shook her head to clear it and regain focus. John asked "Ms. Adesokan, I mean Sharon. Where are the kids?" Sharon opened the door a bit wider and said they are taking a nap. the two kids were sleeping on the floor in the hallway, their coats, and hats still on.

John thought quickly and asked for the rest of the concentrate back because his mother had mistakenly thought they had more in the cupboard. To which Sharon agreed. she turned around slowly almost falling to the side, she giggled and muttered something to herself then walked to the kitchen. John watched her giant butt swish from side to side under her robe. "Dam, he whispered," a couple of minutes went by, and Sharon return to the door and handed John what was left of the "Robo" it was enough to help him get over the hump until he was able to get him a fix of the real deal. John quickly tucked the bottle in his short pocket and ran back down the driveway to his backyard. John went up his stairs and into his backdoor and into his kitchen running to his room shutting the door behind him twisting the top to the "Robo" and taking a big gulp of the liquid. John paused hoping that the neighbor's kids would be okay. But he was then distracted by the memory of Sharon's giant booty. Shaking his head, "dam!" he said under his breath before hopping into his bed and letting the "Robo" take effect.

John began to nod off. His eyelids opened and closed involuntarily. Light and darkness flickers, and with every switch from dark to light John began to dream, suddenly there was the jungle floor, the smell of fresh Mud and wood gave John a vibrant sensation that made him feel more alive. The different animals call to each other to alarm some of the guests in the jungle and others were mating calls for potential suiters echoed through the leaves that hung from giant tree limbs that stretch and intertwined with one another creating a canopy where little light passed through. The beams of light that we're able to weave its way through lit a path to which John crept slowly. John took death breathes of the fresh jungle scent trekking through on the path he noticed a clearing up the way as he approached, he could the sound sounds of congas and voices chanting in a language he had not heard before the deep pounding began to syncopate with the beat of his heart John could feel the earth beneath his feet soften with each step closer. John reached the clearing he saw his father beating feverishly on a giant gold drum. John's' father's face morphs from happy to sad back to happy then to crying back to a giant smile. He was surrounded by others with masks on they beat similar drums all in the same rhythm of John's heartbeat. Suddenly John was startled at the quick appearance of the strange man who came to John when he was in the police car. His eyes were on fire he spoke to John. He said "your path awaits you, beyond the chemical illusion"

Then he reached out to John, John turned away and tried to run but the strange man grabbed John's arm. John struggled as the man's mouth grew wide, he continued to pull John closer the man's teeth turned to fangs dripping blood they got larger as he pulled John closer. the man had turned into a large monster with a hawk's head, human torso, and horses' body. it was preparing to eat John. John squirmed and screamed as he could feel the fangs pierce the top of his head. Just then John jumped up waking from a terrifying nightmare and yelling out to no one.

John lay there drenched in sweat. His chest rose, up and down as he tried to catch his breath. What the fuck? He asked himself. That was too real he mumbled shaking his head in disbelief. John then lifted himself from the cold wet sheets. he walks slowly to the mirror peering deep into his eyes a flash of the image of the strange man shot through his mind, but the fire was in John's eyes this time. John looked at himself with a feeling of contempt. A nothing ass junky, he whispered to his refection. Your father is ashamed of you, he was strong and mighty, but you are weak and a slave to the dope. John's' eyes bulged and began to fill with water. For the first time, he could feel that his father was looking down on him in disgust and not only his father but all his ancestors.

The weight of this reality knocked John to his knees. The despair made him sob deeply. "I'm sorry Mungu" he whimpered. Then the familiar uneasiness of his stomach started to grow from deep in his gut. John knew that he was going to get sick if he did not cop some "H" soon. He managed to climb up onto the sweat-soaked cold sheets and gather his emotions.

Once his mind was clear he got up and found some clothes. He got dressed and headed to the streets to find a new connection for his dope habit. The air was brisk this morning. A bit colder than usual, the sun was still shining even though the news says that rain is coming soon. John paused at the thought of rain, he liked the rain. it always added to his experience when he was high. He would imagen himself as John Coltrane or Charlie Parker pulling back the veil of this superficial existence. John would often play jazz music as the soundtrack to his drift into dreamland. Each note carried him slowly to the next one down the yellow brick road to an emerald-colored bliss.

As John walked the street in search of his fix, he was becoming worried that he might not score and that could lead to the binges. that is a junkie's nightmare, and you ain't got to be sleep for that shit. With each step. John's legs seemed a bit more noodle-like. His knees began to creek like old door hinges desperately in need of oil. John grinned slightly remembering a scene from the movie "The Wiz" John thought, I'm like that dam tinman. John's stomach rumbled on cue as he searched all the spots but with no luck. "Shit!" John exclaimed. He began to scratch himself from the itching sensation deep under his skin.

Jolts of cold chills shot down his spine causing him to twitch. To people who passed by, it looked as if John had lost control of himself. scratching, twitching, and shivering. He had to get to some dope and fast. John walked faster toward 54th street to the "Pink house" this was a spot where all the neighborhood players and gangsters from west and north Oakland would gather it was a neutral place where friends could hang out without the street politics. It was also known as a place to copped whatever your drug of choice may be.

The house is situated on the corner of 54th and Genoa Street. John trotted to the house his body screaming out for relief. He scurry up the chipped grey steps to a black gate that separated the door from the porch. John pressed a small white button to the right of the gate he could hear a faint buzzing sound from behind the front door. A few seconds went by and then John pressed the button again holding it down a bit longer to express the urgency of his visit.

After a couple of tries with no results, John went around the back, to a brown gate. John listened and he could hear the loud music coming through the cracked patio door. John yelled "aye, yooo!" he hears someone from inside say "hey man I think somebody is in the backyard. John was relieved he had gotten the attention of somebody. After a minute or so a group of young people filed out of the house. They all greeted John with nods and waves, as one young man unlocked the brown gate.

John came bursting through the gate twitching ferociously saying to one young man, in particular, "say, Mont, you got some boogie down brown?" to which Mont replied, "bro, you got to quit all that wiggling around me." He continued "that shits making me uncomfortable!" the crowd of young men was now accompanied by a few young ladies who began to laugh at John's inability to control himself. John stood and hugged himself, trying hard to not move so much. but his monkey had become a full-grown Gorilla and it was beating his ass.

John's head went light, and his stomach gurgled and tightened. John said in a muffled voice, come on man do not do me like that." Peeking around at the faces who ridiculed his dope-fiend existence. The young faces reminded him of his ignorance. when he was just seventeen and did not know that the drugs, he played with would eventually play a dirty game of shame on him.

John was dizzy the faces began to blur and just then John could feel the warm liquid bubble up his throat. John clenched his mouth, but it was too late he vomited into his hand the greenish-red liquid burst from between his fingers spraying in every direction some of the spray hit the young girls as they screamed in horror.

All the young kids ran back into the house some gagging from the sight and smell. John could not do anything, his body locking in convulsions as all the food and water violently escaped his body. John went to his knees heaving til nothing, but the sound came out. John was left on his hand and knees crying like a child.

Then two small red balloons drop beside him in the vomit. It was Mont. He had felt sorry for John. Mont knows what it was like to have that monkey attack you. But Mont had been smart enough to shake the drug off and never look back. Even at the early age of fifteen.

John looked at the balloons then at Mont. John grabbed the dope while raising to one knee throw up still dripping from his chin, he then eventually stood and thanked Mont. Mont replied, "man fuck you, you supposed to be an example for us, but you ain't shit." John was frozen with embarrassment. His embarrassment quickly turns to fear as he realized Mont was clutching a small handgun off to his side. John raised his hands and pleaded with Mont "Now hold on youngster, I'll clean up the back yard" John said begging. Mont's eyes watered as he raised the gun to John's stomach and slowly started to squeeze the trigger. the gun's hammer sliding back, mont's finger quivering over the trigger. when a voice came from inside the house "Mont, boy ain't no sense in killing a dead man!" followed by laughter. Then a large shadow appeared in the back doorway behind a thin urine stain bed sheet used as a curtain.

The makeshift curtain slides back to reveal O.G. M-dog. M-dog was one of the older cats who used to run the street way back in the day, but he had gotten caught during a botched robbery turn homicide and he was sentenced to thirty years in Prison. He had just gotten out six months ago and now he was staying with the women who owned the pink house. "I said put that mutha fucking gun away lil nigga, before I take it and shove it up yo ass" M-dog barked. Mont turned slowly towards M-dog and stared at him defiantly. M-dog took a step out of the doorway flexing the muscle he had cultivated for over thirty years in California penal institution. Mont slowly lowers the gun.

Mont looked at John as he walked away and said. "you a lucky bitch." Mont walked into the home's back door followed by M-dog. John stood there clutching the vomit-soaked balloons watching as M-dog and Mont disappeared into the house. John left the back yard headed for home which was only a couple of blocks up genoa from the pink house. John could hear the young people laughing in his head, he kept replaying the whole scene. He saw the faces and the disgust on them. he wishes he had never tried heroin.

John stopped and looked up at the sky. the sun had reached a meridian height and its rays shot down on John's forehead as John begged the sky to release him from this hellish addiction. John screams "please have mercy on me...please!" John stare directly into the sun until it burned his eyes John again found himself on his knees, but this time he was praying. John prayed hard and deep right there on the corner of fifty-fifth and Genoa in front of buddy's clean cuts barbershop

All the barbers and customers were staring out the window wondering what was going on. John just continued to pray. Until he heard a voice whispering to him it said, "hey man ill trade you." John ignored the first attempt he thought it was one of the people in the shop trying to be funny. John was determined to hear from either God or his own ancestors and he was not leaving until then, even if it meant he would be hauled off to jail. John had, had enough.

The voice shot again this time louder "HEY MAN, I SAID I'D TRADE YOU!" John looked up to see the strange bum he had seen at the police car window last night. John hurried to his feet saying, "aww shit what the hell do you want man? can't you see I'm having a freaking mental break down here?" John still holding the balloons he got from Mont tightly in his hand. The strange man said, "I can see a lot of things" he continued "I can hear rather good too!" John stared confused. The strange man went on. "Look, you got something I want, and I think I have exactly what you need" the Man pointed at John's hand. John raised his hand and opened it. The man smiled brightly showing his bottom row of sparkling gold teeth.

John was really confused now because the strange man looked like a bum. so how does he afford a gold grill? It seemed to John that if the strange man was a bum, he would have pawned them for food or dope by now. The Man stepped back and said, "Oh I get it, you too much of a big-time stud to trade with a bum like me huh?" John replied "trade what? What you got for me, man I am dope sick and this shit here is the only cure." The strange man said in a long drawl "shiiiiiiid, lil nigga that ain't no dope. Look a here," the strange bobbed and swayed slightly while opening his hand he said, "this here thang I got will turn you upside down and all the way around, can you dig it?" the stranger opened his hand wider to show John four gold balloons. John looked down as they sparkled in the sunlight. John was skeptical. However, something about the strange man was believable almost hypnotizing.

the strange man whispered something in a weird language, but John did not understand. and before John know it, he had exchanged the red balloons for the gold ones. John was stunned. He was completely baffled by the trick.

The Strange man laughed heartily. "Young man," he said you are about to be free, but freedom comes with duty. And you must be up for the task. John stepped back unsure of what the strange man was talking about. John looked down at the balloons, squeezing them he thought "it feels like any other balloon of dope I had felt before." Then the strange man leaned back slightly with one hand on his hip. he posed like a Musketeer from the Alexandre Dumas book. He was dressed like a typical bum, all raggedy and dusty, however, he seemed regal and royal standing there with a glowing silver silhouette attached to him.

he tilts his head slightly to the sun and spoke

"Some have called me 'Supreme G' but even more know me as 'Willie Sharp' but allow me to reintroduce myself my name is Salamander."

John was confused, he looked back down at the gold balloons and instantly got angry. Throwing the balloons to the ground he said to Salamander "hey old nigga, what the fuck is this bullshit?" John ferociously continued "I thought you were giving me some better dope than what I had, but you trying to give me some way-out hippy shit that's going to have me out here fucked up like you." "I do not want this Hippy Trippy uptown Berzerkely mess. Give me my dope back!!" Salamander slowly brought his chin from the sky gazing sinisterly. he looked John directly in his eyes. "ohhhh, it is dope young man, the finest, most potent skag around this badass town." Salamander changed positions sliding his feet and gracefully contorting his body like a soulful ballet dancer from the Alvin Ailey dance theater. He said son "you have been chosen, and once you chose you can't be "un-chose," he giggled and continued "ya see, it is written in the celestial book of our universal subconsciousness." John wanted to leave but Salamander held his attention by waving his fingers like a caterpillar's legs creating a glowing ball of light and then another four gold balloons appeared in Salamander's palm. John was now frightened, this was no dam bum, he thought to himself. John turned to run deciding to forget about the dope but as he turned to walk away, he noticed something in his hand. John looked down to find the four gold balloons had magically reappeared in his hand.

John began to run this time tossing the balloons into the street. He ran as fast as could towards home. Reaching his front porch, he rushed inside through the front door into the Livingroom, past the photo of Mungu into the hallway, and left to his room opening slamming his door shut behind him.

John was breathing hard, sweat pouring down his face. John assumed he was having a mental breakdown from the heroin binge. Which had seemed to subside while talking to Salamander but now had grown back to the full-sized gorilla that was kicking his ass at the pink house. John felt a sharp pain in his stomach, he double over and then fell to his knees and then over to his side. John felt like his temperature was well over one hundred degrees as he rived in blinding pain. his muscles ached and cramped; intrusive thoughts began to crowd his mind. He thought of suicide briefly before urinating on himself. He felt he was going to throw up, he went to cover his mouth and was shocked to see he had the balloons in his hand again! John was in so much agony that he did not even question how. He just knew he had to stop the pain and so he managed to pop one balloon open and making a fist John poured the contents onto the back of his hand just above the thumb. the powder was glowing white and seemed to have multicolored sparkling crystals in it. John stuck his right nostril into the small mount. Sniffing as hard as could. Then John took the other balloon, popped it, place it on his fist, and sniffed deep. John slowly looked up at the ceiling his eyes filled with tears, his pain reached a crescendo and started to subside.

He finished the last of the sparkly dope. He crawled on his hands and knees like a wounded spider to his dresser. lifted himself up and stared at his ghost-like reflection in the mirror. He noticed his tears streaming down his face, looked like tiny rivers and were now neon orange, his skin glowed like a blacklight poster and had become darker and more beautiful like the people of South Sudan.

John could hear congas beating faintly in his head. His skin crawled as a warm breeze slid over his body and goosebumps appeared all down his arms as the hairs stood up like roses to the sun. Then in the reflection of the mirror vines began to grow out of the walls into his room.

John quickly turned around to see that his room was turning dark as more vines grew out of the four corners into long vines with large leaves exploding from them as they covered the entire floor and walls the ceil melted behind the vines and revealed the night's sky. the congas beat grew in volume the groove became louder as a small path opened. John suddenly remembered the dream he had, and this was the same. The drugs he thought had caused him to hallucinate. John turned back to the mirror but now it had become a large tree stump. The congas thumped in a low thudding continuous rhythm accompanied by hypnotic melodic chanting and rhythmic shouts of ecstasy.

Animals in the distance added vibrant textural noises to the experience. John floated up the path his feet barely touching the cold grassy walkway, and again he found himself face to face with his father Mungu. This time Mungu was focused on John. His eyes were wide and glowing as he sat on a thrown made of bamboo lined with gold and precious jewels that shined in the dark night.

A crown sat atop Mungu's head its material was so reflective it was a world unto itself like you could put your finger through it. At the front of the crown was a symbol a circle with a large v in the middle of it. John just stood there as all the other people came out from behind the trees and high jungle bushes. they were Men and women who John felt he knew, but he did not remember ever meeting them.

They began to take what seemed like fixed positions in the small area. one large man sat to the south another much older man sat to the west directly opposite Mungu's thrown. But to the left of John. Both men had golden collars made of what looked like human bones.

The other people took seats around the perimeter of the small space. In the center John noticed a large stone cube rise from the ground. A woman, one of two who were positioned on Mungu's left and right sides, approached the stone. she carried a large book in her hands. Once she made it to the stone, she placed the large book on the stone flat service top.

She then took a step back and made a sign with her right hand saluting Mungu. Mungu returned the solute and the woman returned to her seat at the right of Mungu. Then the woman on the left rose and she too approached the stone. When she arrived at the stone, she made the same solute as the other women, the solute was given back, she bent down slightly over the large book and gently opened it using only her fingertips. The book's contents were a language of strange symbols and odd signs. Again, the solute was given and returned however this time Mungu said something in a language John had never heard let alone understood.

Instantly the woman floated towards John until she was face to face with him. her scent wafted up John's nose tickling his nostril hairs causing his knees to weaken, her hair which extended down to the back of her thighs were thick Locs with gold clips sectioning off every foot of its length. her beautiful dark skin shimmering as she swayed from side to side so close to John that he could feel the tiny hairs of her arms stroking his, before turning her back to him. her large behind wobbled to a stop. She began to step to the slow buttery mystic rhythms of the congas that had been continuously pounding into the night's sky. her moves were intense, fluid, and sensual. She danced a pattern first toward the older man in the west rolling her hips in a snake-like pattern with every step, and then to the man seated in the south. She slowly made her way back to the stone. She opened the book and stopped. She then gave the solute which was returned by Mungu at which point everyone stood and celebrated her dancing with shouts and tribal noises. The woman returned to her place and took her seat. John was hypnotized by the whole scene his eyes glazed over like white pearls. He jumped, as he was startled by a hand placed on his shoulder. Turning to see Salamander, he was dressed in a long black robe that went down to the ground. He held a staff that was at least 8 feet tall with a representation of the earth at its tip. John went to speak but was quickly silenced by Salamander. Then Salamander guided John gently to turn around completely so that John and salamander were now facing out of the small space with everyone else behind them. With Salamander's hand still on John's shoulder Salamander led John backward into the space. With every step backward he whispered to John "ujue nafsi yako hatufi" which means *know your soul, we do not die.'*

As the congas began to get louder and the chants more passionate, the women sang a song that mixed in the other sounds. The birds cried out and flew in and out of the small space. A Black Panther crept stealthily past the stone as salamander and John moved backward in a zig-zag pattern around the stone and large book. A burst of fire spout from the mouth of each of the women who sat aside Mungu. John's heartbeat rapidly. The ground under John's feet grew soft and moist. Salamander continued to lead John backward "ujue nafsi yako hatufi" he said until John felt the irresistible urge to repeat the words they slip from John's slightly opened lips. The words seemed to come from deep in John's chess his now bounding like a gorilla trying to punch his way out. Then everything and everyone moved in unison in ultra-slow motion. the small animals walked through the small space the Black

Panther climbed into a tree and rested on its limb which hung over Mungu's thrown while the people dance wildly to the congas echoing in the jungle night. Every being had become one, and John was brought to the center of it all. Salamander and John stood with their back turned to the stone and large. Salamander removed his hand from John's shoulder, letting John know that the rest of the journey would have to be taken alone. Then Salamander told John "Turn and face your god" John's body began to turn before John could think about moving. Once he was fully turned around, he looked up at the thrown, and to his surprise, he saw himself. The figure on the thrown smiled at John and said "we don't die, we are forever" you have received the key and engaged in the ceremony of discovering the secret curtain, and now do you wish to peek behind it? John answered yes! I am. John's voice was deep and unlike it had been before like it did not belong to him. the figure on the thrown with John's face rose and floated down to the stone and large book, where John was standing. once there he reached his hand out to John. John's left hand rose slowly, the figure grasped John's hand tightly with his right hand and pulled a small dagger out. the Black panther that rested on the limb let out a low growl that vibrated through John's body. the figure plunged the dagger into John's palm, but John felt no pain and there was no blood only light protruded from the hole in John's hand. The figure exclaims to John this is all that we are, The Light! The figure shouted. the crowd still slowly dancing to the congas beat repeated "The Light!" John whispered "the light" the figure returned removed the dagger and returned to the throne where he sat, face now back to Mungu's. "God is the light, and the light is all that there is, and we are a part of this Light." We exist because it exists. without it, we do not come to be. Our shells leave us time and time again, but we return to the light only to re-emerge into the covering of life. This my son is the secret, and now you may live with this great secret and protect it from those who are not worthy of it. John bowed slightly and thanked Mungu.

Mungu rose again and said "before you go, there's something else. He continued "you are free, and it is now your duty to free others even if it means you must give up your own covering!" John frowned and replied "wait, what? Do you mean Like a superhero or something? Suddenly the ground began to shake, and the crowd of dancers and spectators quickly retreated into the jungle as the large book slammed shut and the stone sunk back into the ground. the leaves and vines instantly melted together and receded as John's room transformed back to its regular state. Signaling the trip was over.

☀ ☀ ☀

VI

Chapter 6

LIFE AFTER DEATH

When John came back to this consciousness, he was standing on top of his bed. He looked at his mirror to see his naked body. John then looked down to see that his feet were covered with light brown mud. John then crumbled down as if he had been robbed of his spine. He giggled hysterically as he thought "wow, that was some kinda' trip. This dope here is Pow...Wah... full!" but the glee dissipated as John wiggled his toes remembering his muddy feet. Wait this is impossible. I know I was high but Goddam, did I walk outside? Where did this mud come from? He pondered for a minute but then he shrugged off his thoughts and figured he must have walked outside without his shoes and socks. that would explain the jungle hallucination. It was his backyard, right! That's it, it is just one big freaky trip. John gasped, raising his hand to his mouth, hoping he had not gone outside butt naked. A sense of fear came over John. "Fuck!" he whispered sharply. The blaring green glow of John's clock digits displayed 7:35

am this made John feel a little better if he was outside with his nuts out at least most people were sleeping or still eating breakfast, so they probably didn't see him. John rose and grab a pair of shorts and went to the bathroom to take a shower.

As John entered the bathroom, he noticed something slightly odd. he felt strange like something was missing. John stepped in front of the mirror. Placing his hands on the opposite edges of the cold white sink and leaning into the streak-free mirror. It hit him like lighting through a tree. He was not sick and in fact, he had no urges to cop any heroin. John just stared deeply focused on the image in the mirror. The sink was dripping water droplets in two-second increments. the subtle sound became a crashing boom at the bottom of the white sink and echoed around the dead silent bathroom. Bloop.... Bloop.... Bloop! "clarity," John thought "I haven't been this clear-headed in years." He silently admitted to himself.

He lowered his gaze to the water drops concentrating on each drop until the drops began to move slower. John focused even more and after a few minutes' John realized that he was staring at a drop of water suspended in mid-air.

John gripped in fear and confused slowly stood up straight. The droplet still floating. John turned to his right to see a shadow outside the bathroom-treated window. John rushed to the window twisted the lock and opened it. No one was there John stuck his head out the window looking both ways to make sure it was not someone hiding. He looked to the left, up the neighbor's driveway adjacent to his house. then he looked right and to his surprise, there was salamander standing at the front of the driveway leaning against a large tree that overhung its entrance.

Salamander grinned and called out "hey Johnny my boy, come and see the sights, Champ!" John yelled back "Man, what the fuck you are doing here?" "Fuck I'm doing here?" Salamander shot back, then continued. "Hell, I'm here to help you on your journey fool." To which John said "what mutha fuckin journey?" there was a pause and then salamander exclaimed "the Journey we all must take in order to become who we were meant to be sucka! now bring yo' custy ass on outside and let me talk to you like a civilized human being, Goddamit." John quickly slides his head back inside the bathroom window slamming it shut and locking it back. John rushed to turn on the water and noticed the droplet was still floating. John reached out and touched the droplet, it popped and ran down his fingertips and down the scratched surface surrounding the sink's drain. John quickly washed his feet removing the mysterious mud.

Once outside John approached Salamander and attempted to shake his hand but was abruptly stopped. Salamander said "check this out youngster, from here on out the shits about to get thick. I'm talking elephant shit thick! Can you dig it?" John was unsure of what was going on. John had a bunch of questions he needed answered. John shook his head up and down and reluctantly mumbled "yeah." Salamander smiled cartoonishly wide and said in a slick southern drawl "Well, well, well ain't you just the good ole' agreeing type a niggah" Salamander stumble back a few steps laughing uncontrollably then he stopped and went into a dance step like he was a backup for the Temptations or New Edition or something like that.

John just stood there; his face frowned up with confusion. As Salamander dipped and bopped from side to side spinning around then sliding backward all the while grunting and singing some unintelligible lyrics from an unknown song. "Hey!" John said trying to get Salamander's attention with no results. "Hey, hey, Heeeeey old Niggah! John shouted, "Cut out all that weird-ass shit, and tell me what's going on; shit." John said angrily. Salamander froze then he looked up at John and said, "okay I see you can't dig the slick and savvy moves of "Pimptitutde," huh?" fixing his old clothes and straightening his bright red ascot handkerchief that wrapped around his neck. Salamander cleared his throat as if he were preparing to make a speech. He said, "Say baby" he started out in a smooth song-like tone. "You remember that dope I lay on you yesterday? Huh, do ya? Salamander continued "well that wasn't no or... din... nary... shit, baby."

Salamander took John by the elbow and turned him gently as he said, "come on brother let's take a walk." they started down 56th St. headed west towards Genoa. the air was crisp, as it whipped around John's face. The Sun seemed brighter than it had been in recent days. Salamander began his talk "first things first, your father is alive and well" John stiffened at the news, but Salamander quickly detoured his reaction and continued his speech. "He is in another place beyond what you can see and hear at this present time. But you will be reunited with him soon." Salamander continued his sparkling bloodshot eyes focused on John's face, watching for micro-movements. "Recently there was a battle in which a doorway to his location was opened. we will go there but first, you must learn to see."

After a long slow stroll through the neighborhood salamander and John approached a cherry red Cadillac Brougham. Salamander leaned gently on the front hood of the shiny chariot. He grinned slightly revealing that his bottom row of gold teeth had become even more bright. "This world is a playhouse my boy, and we are the dolls the Gods animate." John stared perplexed. Salamander spoke sharply in a serious tone, "wipe that dumbass look off yo' face boy " switching positions raising one leg, placing it halfway on the top of the hood. His long shoe dangling off the side. Listen you are not like everybody else around here. Yes, you used dope like it was water, and I understand it was to cope with the pain of losing your father However, there is more to your story baby bubba. You come from a family of Magi. They have been running from some seriously Evil People for ages until the One was finally trained in the way of the Rahsan Clan.

Now the war is raging, and it is your time to get involved. John Held out his hand to stop Salamander in mid-sentence. He said "look man, I'm grateful for the dope you gave me. I feel great and I'm not tweaking or even feel like I want more, but you got to miss me with all the Funkadelic, sir nose de 'void of funk, and the adventures of Dr funkinstein type shit you running down on me dude." John continued "I'm not some Geek from off the street, I know my way around this town. You not gonna con me into playing some weird fantasy game with you, old man... can you dig it?"

Salamander slid off the car slowly, adjusted his ascot, and walked around to the trunk of the car. Never taking his eyes off John he reached down into his coat pocket and retrieved a set of gold keys. After finding the right one, he used it to open the trunk. The trunk obscured John's view and after a minute salamander popped his head out from behind the glittering trunk. "Come here nigga." Salamander said in a low stern tone. John hesitantly walked over to see what was there. when John finally investigated, he saw a brown box trimmed in gold. It had strange hieroglyphics covering it and a glowing light that came from the crack of the lid. Salamander said, "I get it, you think you were high and hallucinating last night, right?" John Nodded. "of course, that shit you gave me was laced, with some craziness!" just as John finished his reply Salamander opened the box the bright light gave way to large vines growing out of its center. John leaped back gripped with fear. As the green goldish glowing vines crept out of the box slithering around the trunk and the smooth waves and tiny sprouting leaves created a fractal design that hypnotized John., his pupils dilated revealing large black pits set dead center of his yellowish-white bulging eyes. Bam! Went the trunk as Salamander shove the hood down with vicious intent, severing the stage one sleep state that the veins produced in John's Brain. "You think this is a game?" Salamander asked loudly "they have your father, are you going to let him disappear from your memory and live in a hellish eternity of the forgotten Gods?" John regained his faculties and responded, "please old dude, explain to me what the fuck is going on!" John continued "have I lost my mind, is any of this real?" before Salamander could answer John took off running down the street. John ran back up MLK Blvd. and then north towards Berkeley finally reaching 61st where he made a left. He ran past Edward Roe who laughed at John, as he ran down the block. Ed thought to himself "what a waste" then he screamed out "hey slow down dope fiend ass nigga, that heroin at going nowhere." John did not even turn around he just ran to his uncle's house.

☀ ☀ ☀

823 61ˢᵗ street a two-story home where his uncle and cousins lived. John's burst through the front door and locked it behind him John was pacing back and forth in the Livinggroom as his uncle Sonnie B, stared confused. John tried to catch his breath as his cousin Jamal and Dame played dominoes. They did not even seem to notice John who by this time had fallen on the old couch adjacent to the door. John's chest heaved up and down as he tried to catch his breath. Domino! Dame yelled excitingly as Jamal turned over his hand to reveal the points, he would have to give Dame, 5,10,15 Jamal counted. He then reached for the pencil and wrote the sum on a notepad.

Dame began flipping over the Dominos he looked over at John finally acknowledging his presents. "Whuts up lil nigga?" Dame shouted across the Livingroom. Dame was at least two feet shorter than John but since John was the youngest of all his cousins he would have to submit to the title of Little. John eased up straightening himself on the couch and replied "man, I'm in some shit!" Jamal and dame looked at each other, and then back at John. Jamal then asked, "what happen, you tried to rob somebody for some dope, and now they bouts ta beat yo ass?" John instantly felt the sting of embarrassment as Jamal, Uncle Sonny, and Dame all doubled over with laughter. John Quickly shot back "hey! this is serious" the room fell silent. then in a crybaby accent mocked John "hey, this is serious you guys!" to which three went back to loud laughter and knee-slapping" John was growing frustrated he knew he was in something that just could not be ignored. Uncle Sunny noticed that John was not laughing and had an unusual look in his eyes. He noticed that John had somehow gained some weight since the last time he saw him and that was odd because dope fiends do not gain weight. Uncle sonny hushed Jamal and Dame. They both got quiet. "Nephew, you good have you been in the gym?" to which John replied "No, Unc" he continued "but that is what I am trying to tell you I ain't on drugs no more!" the three were stunned Jamal was the first to ask, "dude you got clean, but shit you acting like you in trouble." Dame chimed in "yeah dude that's a good thing ain't it?" John stood up and said, "okay just listen, and I'll tell you what happened" John began to run down the last couple of days he talked about the police killing spooky-man and the strange bum who gave him the Magic dope. Uncle Sunny, Jamal, and Dame just sat there in disbelief the four of them sat there for five minutes staring at the Television. Chuck Johnson's Soul Beat a local black tv network was on. Luenell a comedian from the area was hosting her call-in show when the phone rang. "Hello, you're on the air baby!" luenell said with a slur due to one too many Hennessy and cokes. "Hello, caller is you there, baby?" "Yeah, I'm here, have no fear!" the caller answered. "Hey now, have no fear. Who do I have the pleasure of speakin' to?" luenell inquired. the voice on the other end replied, "why I am the rootabaw, pootabaw, some say some saw" the caller continued "I am up, I am down in every city and town, I am the Suckers' slander and the women's commander...I am the Majestic Magician aka, Salamander!" John leaped to his feet "that's him he shouted" pointing at the T.V. "that is the dude who gave me the magic dope. Just then Lunell's face went blank. She then looked up as if she were looking into the camera and out at John. The caller then said "there ain't no place to run, John" "John, Mutha fucka my name is luenell!" the tipsy host exclaimed. "You trying to say I sound like a goddam man?" she shouted "I'm hanging up on you Mr. Pander, Jammer scammer whatever yo' fuckin name is. Bye!" John turned and rushed to the front door but just as he grabbed the knob to open it three loud knocks came crashing from it. John stopped in his tracks. Dame reach under the table, that he and Jamal were seated at and pulled a long rifle out. He aimed at the door. Simultaneously Uncle Sunny pulled a 357 magnum from under the couch cushion, Jamal retrieved a handgun from a nearby drawer situated behind him. "Move yo ass out the way boy" Uncle sunny whispered to John. John slowly stepped back to give everyone a clear shot at the door. "Who the fuck is it?!" Uncle Sonny shouted while aiming the long barrow at the entrance. There was silence. sweat gathered on John's forehead as the tension of the moment grew. Then a voice broke the void "it's me, Ed roe, hell yall doing in there, beaten' ya meats?" A sigh of relief could be heard from all four of them. Dame rushed to the door and opened it to let Ed roe in. "bruh why the hell is you knockin' so dam hard fo'? you scared the shit out of us, man!" Ed walked in giggling "My Bad yall" he said jovially "I was just coming to tell yall that some cat is outside looking for John. All four men stared at one another. "where" uncle sonny said while pulling the front curtain back slightly and peeking out with one eye. He noticed a long car parked at the curb in front of the house. Uncle Sonny signaled to John waving him over to check it out. To John's surprise, it was Salamander's car. The phone rang, Jamal turns to his side where the receiver vibrated next to him. it rang five times before Jamal picked it up. "Who dis?" Jamal impatiently asked. "Why it is I," the voice on the other end said in a relaxed melodic tone. The voice continued "Jamal, put John on the phone." Jamal jumped back with fright throwing the phone at John saying, "here nigga it's for you!" the phone tumbled to John's foot as John reached down to pick it up the front door slammed shut and Salamander appear in the corning of the Livingroom Ed Roe screamed "oh shit, I see you niggas is busy, I will come back later!" and ran to the door. He tried to open it, but the knob was stuck "what the fuck, is going on!?" Ed yelled. By this time Dame aimed his rifle at Salamander and squeezed the trigger but nothing happened. Jamal and Uncle Sonny went to shoot their guns and again only clicks of their hammers could be heard. Salamander reached in his coat pocket pulling out a long Joint. Putting it to his lips he proceeded to light it. Taking a long pull as the substance burned brighter lighting up the dim corner. "Are you niggas done?" Salamander asked sarcastically. Allow me to introduce myself. Cutting Salamander off abruptly, Uncle cried out "we know who the fuck you are, you're the devil and my nephew messed up and sold his soul to you." Salamander burst into a heavy Laugh, choking a little on the joint's smoke and he then cleared his throat before saying "I can assure you Sonny; I am not a devil in any sense of the word." He continued "Have a seat Gentleman, while I run it down to you" Salamander waved his hand directing the five men to sit. Four of them followed the gesture and sat on the long brown couch and one on the "lazy boy" chair that sat opposite the long couch. Salamander took a step forward with his right foot and then placed his left foot's hill inward towards the right one creating a shape. The five-man looked on compelled by fear and enchantment. Salamander once again wave his hands but this time it was not to give direction, he waved his hands in a circle slowly manifesting a light. He then told the five to look into the light. Salamander began to tell a story of another realm and a man who was banished into a frozen place in that realm, and how that man become a scourge on the minds of the people who had banished him. this scourge's name was Hsub and he was known to appear and kill these people. The people were known as the Rahsan Clan. the Rahsan were an ancient people. it is said that they have been in existence since the great San "Created himself out of himself" but once Hsub appeared from the frozen lands with his army of evil. He scattered the Rahsan to four corners of their realm and once there was nowhere to hide there the Rahsan people began to hide here in this realm as well as others. In fact, there are some Rahsan who can even jump to different realms and time periods. John spoke up asking "you mean like the future and past? "To which salamander quickly answered "Exactly" then John responded, "well why not go back to before the banishment and kill Hsub?" salamander seemed agitated by the silly question. he answered through clenched teeth "don't you think they would have tried that by now fool?" the room was silent for a moment and then salamander continued "look, this is not some fantasy or figment of your imagination, this is reality, Your reality!" your father is Rahsan and that makes you Rahsan. You all are Rahsan even though Ed is not of biological relation. all Rahsan find each other Naturally and form bonds that are unbreakable even after death because no one ever really dies. Now let us get down to why I have summoned you. John sat straight up, now focusing even most intently on Salamander's words. "As I have said before John, your father is in fact alive and trapped in the other realm and there's more your grandfather is there as well." "My grandfather I've never even heard of him before today" John answered excitedly. "Yes, your grandfather who was chief of our village before Hsub sent his army to raid our homeland and we had to escape." Salamander paused before continuing seemingly lost in the memory. "Your grandfather came to this Realm and stayed in Northeast Africa where he met your grandmother. your father was then born not long after. Salamander slowly turned to Sonny and said, "you were just a baby when we came here." You do not have any memory of the other realm. We thought it would be best to not tell you since we were in hiding. If you did not know then you could not tell anyone who might have been working for Hsub and the Nashar. For the next few months, we will have to develop each of your skillsets and then we will produce a plan to go into the other realm and rescue your father and grandfather. We will start first thing in the morning" then Salamander clapped his hands, and the room went dark for a second or two and when the lights came back on Salamander was gone.

☀ ☀ ☀

VII

Chapter 7

THE STORY OF AURIM

The following morning John awoke to the popping sounds of frying lamb chops. The delicious smell filled the Livingroom. John sat for a minute trying to recall the right before and put it into a more digestible chain of events Dame and Jamal sat at the kitchen table talking about Salamander and the coming training. "Man, I'm gone be the rawest magician in history," Jamal said while moving his fingers in a conjuring motion. Dame laughed and replied "shit, you mean you gone be a niggagician" everyone laughed. John walked in from the Livingroom and sat at the table with dame and Jamal. Uncle Sonny was flipping some lamb chops. The popping sound grew louder as the meat was laid gently back into the hot butter. John's stomach rumbled, he was hungry and could not wait to grub on that lamb. "Uncle you almost done over there?" John asked impatiently. "Just about, nephew" uncle sonny replied. Uncle sonny sprinkle some herbs from a shaker and exclaimed "tah dah!" as he spun around holding the large pan with a red mitt on his right hand and a metal spatula in his left. Uncle walked around the table sliding each of the young men a chop onto their plates. An empty plate was set for ed roe who had gone home last night but said he would be back as soon as he woke up. "Ed better hurry up, shit I'm gonna eat his chop too" John jokily shouted to the others. On cue, the door shook from the hard-knocking. Dame jumped from his chair and went to the door, he opened it, and Ed walked in. "what's happening fellas yall ready for this bizarre ride into the Far side?" Ed said playfully he continued "that Salamander dude is a trip, huh?" everyone nodded in agreement. The room fell silent as everybody stare into space flashing back to the night before. There was a tension that could not be denied. Great fear mixed with insatiable inquisitiveness glued their face muscles in melancholy positions as they waited for Salamander to come. At that moment music could be heard from outside. The soul singer Willie Hutches' hit song 'I choose you from the motion picture "the Mack" was blaring. Increasing in volume as it got closer, the bass vibrated the walls of the house. Louder and louder until the pictures that hung, swung, and danced along the walls like the arms of a breakdancer. Then suddenly it stopped. Then shortly after the music stopped, there was a knock at the door. Everyone rushed to the door uncle sonny grabbed its knob and yanked it open. But there was no one there just a long shiny Cadillac glistening in the Sun's light. The sound of a throat being cleared from inside the house startled the men as they quickly turned to see Salamander sitting at the dining room table. His leg crossed over the other. He wore a bright yellow suit with a hat that matched in color. The hat was shaped cowboy style, but it cascaded up to a point like a Wizard's cap. There was a feather that protruded from the buckle of the orange band surrounding the base of the cap slowly wafted in the air with salamanders' slightest movements like a conductor's wand keeping in time to its master's rhythm. He wore big round, shades of yellow in color that hide his eyes. The bottom of his afro puffed from the bottom of his hat looked like a pillow of black cotton. it sparkled slightly as if sprayed with the most expensive bottle Afro sheen had to offer. A large Cuban link chain rested on his neck and draped down to his chess. It had a large medallion made of pure solid gold attached to it, and on it was a circle, within the circle was a V with two lines at its sides. This laid over a bed of diamonds that were exploding with light that boogied across our retinas creating a dream-like display. This set atop his wrinkle-free bright orange shirt that was tucked into yellow pants creased so sharp that a fly flew too close and was sliced in half. His shoes were red and yellow leather hush puppies with diamond tips on the shoestrings.

Everyone stood there admiring the strange display when Ed shouted out "man what the fuck do you have on?" dame, John, and Jamal chuckled nervously. Uncle Sonny quickly replied shit ed your young ass does not know divine style when you see it. Sonny walked over to Salamander Slapping his outreached palm with his own. Then turning his hand over to receive the same.

Salamander grinned and said smoothly "you jive chumps do not know style or a mutha fuckin thing about life for that matter." The guy's chuckles melted into embarrassment. Salamander continued "listen up suckas, I'm going to need you turkeys to get hip and I mean quick. This is not a joke your lives are on the line; can you dig it?" the guys all answered in the affirmative and quickly sat down to listen as their instructor began. Salamander uncrossed his legs and stood up slowly then spun around his chair while pushing it up to the table to clear some space for himself. Sonny moved closer to the others not wanting to miss any part of the coming instructions. Salamander shimmed his shoulder slightly as his bright yellow trench slipped off down his back salamander effortlessly caught it as it fell, he then flipped the coat upward and twisted it in the air he folded it neatly, and placed it on the back of the chair. Now with his manicured fingertips he unfastened his yellow ruby cufflinks and rolled up his sleeves once done he clapped his hands together and said, "Okay which one of you turkeys is going first?" the guys were confused they just stared at salamander trying to figure out the question. Salamander continued with a giggle "well don't fall over yourself rushing" then he repeated himself "which one of you niggas is going first?" Then Ed stood up and said, "fuck it I'll go!" "gooood" salamander said while grinning. Ed walked over to salamander and just as he got within arm's reach salamander tapped ed on his shoulder knocking Ed to the floor. The others were shocked and concerned as to what was going on. Then the old wizard moved his hand in a circular motion the air around the room began to move gently swirling about as ed's body rose from the ground and floated. Ed now four feet off the ground started to glow his eye popped open his eyes sparkled as they darted from person to person. Wow! Ed whispered, "what is this place?" "Guys can you see it, can you see what I'm seeing!" Ed asked with pure excitement. "Blood, what are you seeing?" shouted John. Ed did not answer he just laughed loudly as he floated down until he was no longer glowing and back to his normal self. Ed still giggling said between gasps of air "Man, that was the shit, I want to go back!" then salamander asked, "who next?" and the fellas all raised their hands stumbling over one another to get close to salamander.

John! salamander called. "Please step up and take a seat." John hurried, grabbing a chair from the table, and placing it directly in the front of salamander, and sat down. John wanted to experience what Ed Roe had. Salamander took his seat and reclined slightly. His shoulders relaxed, and a calmness slid across his face. His peculiar grin hinted at a secret, to soon be revealed. Then salamander asked in a smooth deep vibrating voice. "Do you know your history?" John squinted his eyebrows not knowing whether to answer in the affirmative or to say no. John shrugs his shoulders and mumbled "kind of" to which Salamander laughed. "Kinda? what Kinda! Answer is that? Either you do or do not, ain't no kinda, nigga!" John quickly blurted out his new answer No, sir! Salamander sensing John's anxiousness signaled with his diamond-encrusted manicured hand to John with a commanding voice "relax sucka" he continued "let me school you and get ya hip." I have already told you about how we can get to this dimension, but this is how your grandfather and father were captured and taken by Hsub's soldiers. We lived in an area now known as the Central African Republic. We created small settlements and began spreading the ancient secrets amongst our people so that they could build edifices for those of us who would follow from the ether realms, however, this was a mistake because we inadvertently left breadcrumbs for Hsub and his villains to find us. After Decades of living in peace Hsub's sentinels stumble upon our edifices and began raiding our cities. We packed up and ran to land you may know as Ethiopia, but we knew it then as "Kush" it was named after the all-healing cosmic Herb smoked by the shamans of our home realm. It is said that when the Rahsan Smoke the Kush they can see and talk to the ancestors, receiving instructions and guidance. While in Kush we established schools of learning for our people. We lived there for centuries, but just as before, the Hsub's soldiers soon found us. They burned our schools, and a lot of the books and captured most of us. Your grandfather then escaped with the royal family to the land you know as Egypt. But this time we devised a way to hide our identity. We painted our faces and dressed in elaborate costumes and, instead of a language written in our original alphabet we used symbols to conceal and never reveal the truth of who we are. The ancient story of our people is still there today written on all the walls. In fact, the Hsub's Nashar, are there now thousands of years later still trying to decipher the codes to find the other Rahsan in the other realms. I watch them on T.V. every day digging up the graves of our dead to study our remains. They have even found the doorways to the other realms, but they cannot get them to work. They are missing the keys. Your grandfather knew that they would find them again, however, this time they were very prepared so when the time came the Rahsan did not resist. There was no alarm sounded no reaction whatsoever. This confused the Nashar soldiers, they reported back to Hsub that whoever these people were, they cannot be the

Rahsan. This allowed the royal family to slip to the western parts of the African Continent. Great Kingdoms were created by the Rahsan using the same codes disguised in signs and symbols. Only the trusted members of the inner circle were allowed to have books that contained the original text. Later Secret Noble societies were formed. These Societies had members whose goal was to travel into foreign lands and teach those who proved themselves worthy of regaining the knowledge wisdom and understanding of the ancient Rahsan People and of the religion of San. But low and behold this was another mistake. Salamander dropped his head in disappointment his eyes began to fill with tears. As continued. "This was the beginning of the great Nightmare"

Part 2

Aurim

Salamander orders sonny to fix him a glass of Tycoon cognac. Sonny was confused he had never heard of this brand before. He explains to Salamander "I'm sorry but I ain't got that bruh" Salamander just grinned and said, "it's from the future, now just go to where you keep your liquor, and it will be there." Sonny shook his head in disbelief and reluctantly went to his liquor cabinet to his surprise a giant bottle of tycoon cognac was there not only one, but every bottle in his cabinet had changed to tycoon. Sonny yelled, "I'll be Goddam, what is this shit man?" Salamander yelled back in response "Nigga just fix some dranks, and don't worry about it." Sonny had been a bartender for years but was confused he asked, "what do I mix this shit with?" Dame laughed "cola" Salamander answered. Once sonny had fixed the beverages for all the crew. He handed Salamanders his glass. Salamander tipped his glass upwards and toward the crew and said, "We are the blessed of the best" and took a deep gulp of the brown liquid. Then slamming the glass on the table. "Woah!" he exclaimed loudly, as the crew took sips of their drinks. "oooo weee" Jamal whispered, after tasting the sweet beverage. "Buddy, buddy, buddy this is some good shit here." He said while mimicking comedian Richard Pryor's Mud Bone character's voice. John, Dame, Ed, Sonny, and even Salamander began to laugh. Then Salamander waves his hand to quiet the laughter. He took a deep breath and continued the story.

For centuries, the Rahsan had been successful in keeping their identities hidden. The members of the noble society had moved all around the continent of Africa initiating new members. until on an unlucky day the society was discovered by a member of Hsub's offspring. This young man was the result of a hidden affair between a Rahsan female named Caliana-El and Hsub's grandson whom the Nashar called Suseg. Caliana was a beautiful young woman. Her blemish-free dark Chocolate skin shimmered in the light of the great San, and even at night while touched by the Moons illuminating glow. Her large, turquoise-colored eyes captured the attention of all in her presences. She was very tall even for a Rahsan Woman who was known to be above the average height of others in the other realms and although slender her body was extraordinarily voluptuous. At that moment Uncle Sonny yelled out "goddam" slapping his hands together loudly.

Salamander continued. One day while Suseg was on patrol he had heard of a rumor that a small village in what is now known as Sierra Leone was harboring a family of Rahsan. He and his platoon rode into this village and discover the Rahsan family. Suseg ordered his platoon to take all the Rahsan into custody they went home to home looking for the rest of the Rahsan. Suseg burned the home of those who had to hide the Rahsan when he was stopped in his tracks. He entered a home on the outskirts of the village and saw Caliana he was instantly smitten by her beauty so much, so he fell to his knees the torch he was using to ignite the fires fell to the floor causing it to set ablaze. Suseg realizing his mistake leaped to his feet and grabbed Caliana hoisting her up in his pale arms and rushing her out the back way of the home. Since this home was on the outer perimeter, he was able to take into the jungle without being spotted by the platoon. He had never seen such perfecting his mind was torn. He was Nashar and she was an enemy of his people, however, his heart was unable to make such a distinction. He told her to remain in hiding and that he would come back. Caliana was too frightened to refuse, and she knew the alternative was to be captured and killed by the Nashar, so she agreed. Suseg returned to his platoon and gave orders to take the prisoners back to the home realm for execution. Suseg told his soldiers that he would remain behind to see if any more Rahsan would come this way. His lieutenant asked, "sir do you think that it is wise to remain here by yourself?" Suseg stared angrily at his lieutenant and growled "never question my wishes or you will a guest in the gallows along with the Rahsan scum, do you understand?" "Yes! General, I understand" the lieutenant barked back. Then he turns to the platoon and yelled "move out" after the platoon disappear over the horizon. Suseg made his way back into the jungle to where he had left Caliana. He found her there, shivering from fear. He asked her name to which she replied he acknowledge her name as suitable title for such a lovely being. As the great San set and darkness began to glide over the land like honey oozing over a finger Suseg and Caliana talked through the night they both shared their desires and dreams Caliana explaining to Suseg that she did not understand why the Nashar hated the Rahsan so much and that from what she could tell Suseg was a kind-hearted person. Salamander paused to remind the crew that Caliana had not heard Suseg order her family to be put to death. Dame reacts to that fact saying "dam, that's some cold-blooded shit right there." Salamander responded "cold-blooded indeed" then he went back to the story. Eventually falling asleep under the night's sky, the two felt they had been placed together by fate and that they would create a new life without the rules of the Nashar and Rahsan. months past and by this time Suseg had built a small cottage for them to live in. there was plenty of fruit trees and vegetable around to eat from, as well as a river for fishing. Life was looking up for the two outcasts. until one-night Suseg was awoken by the crackle of torches to see his lieutenant holding a long sword to the neck of Caliana. He grinned and said to Suseg "Now I see why you chose to stay behind" Suseg watched the blade sink slightly into Caliana's neck. a dark crimson stream of blood rolled down the shiny blade. Suseg jumping to his feet begged his Lieutenant not to hurt Caliana. Caliana's captor then took the tip of his blade and sliced over the front of her garment revealing a plump belly. The lieutenant seeing this threw Caliana to the ground in disgust he shouted "Suseg, what would your grandfather say if he knew you were a committing such an atrocious and vile act?" he went on, "and to plan to bring an impure creature by a Rahsan monster into existence?" I cannot allow such a thing, the lieutenant raised his sword and began to down with great force on to head of Caliana, the blade swished threw the air, and just before it made its finite blow Suseg leaped into action catching the blade with his bare hand blood bursting from his palm, he tackled the Lieutenant. They fought like two wild beasts growling pouching kicking and biting each other blood began to shower the small cottage as the two men struggle for domination over the other. Until finally a blow was struck, and the victor arose from the melee there on the ground bleeding profusely was Suseg he had been stabbed through the heart. With his last bit of strength, he reached out to Caliana his arm stretched out to her, his fingertips twitching earnestly to close the distance between them only to have them brutally cut off by the lieutenant's bloody sword. There Suseg lay in detached from his hand, his love, and his life. The Lieutenant turned his face slowly towards Caliana his body covered in her lovers' blood as it dripped from his fingertips, he raises his hand and licked the fluid. His face filled with Hatred and Malice. He spoke hauntingly soft "I'm going to cut that monster out of your belly, and I'm going to stomp its head then I'm going to hang your bodies from one of these jungle trees" He took a slow step forward and was startled by the voice of Suseg, "don't!" Suseg begged the lieutenant to turn to Suseg and quickly stabbed him in the neck making sure the blade went into the ground underneath Suseg completing his death. the lieutenant distracted by Suseg's last attempt did not notice Caliana slipping passed him, and when he turned around to complete his horrible task, he was met with the torch he dropped slamming directly into his face. He instantly dropped his sword and tried to put out the flames that had attached themselves to his hair and beard. Caliana quickly picked up the sword and began to slice at the lieutenant. Salamander paused and put emphasis on his next words "Brothers, she cut his ass everywhere, but the bottom of his mutha fuckin' feet." The crew roared into loud uncontrollable laughter. After the wild giggling and knee-slapping had stopped John asked, "so then what happened?"

Salamander caught his breath and proceeded with the rest of the tale. Caliana had killed the lieutenant and was now on the run alone and scared she made her way to another village where she gave birth to her child. The child was named Aurim which meant light. His mother named him that because he was conceived in the darkness of forbidden love.

Caliana knew that any clue to his conception marked him for death. So, after he was born his mother placed him on a camel with a note written in the ancient Rahsan Language that said "too whom the great San gives this gift, receive it well" after weeks in the desert the baby made it to a city called Dhahabu today it's called Johannesburg in South Africa, and this is where I found him. "What?" yelled Ed roe, "you were the one who brought that mutha fucka around our people?" Salamander regretfully answered in the affirmative. He said, "yes, I am the one who found Aurim a regret I have lived with for centuries." Salamander continued I took him to one of many homes and had my Harem of wives raise him as my own. And when it was time, the Noblemen found him. he was among a group of young men who were looked upon as smart, intuitive, and possessed limited but above average spiritual abilities. The nobles befriended this group of bright young men giving them brief glimpses of the ancient magic they possessed with quick words and sleight of hand tricks.

All the boys were intrigued, but none more than Aurim. His eagerness was refreshing to the noblemen and so they showed special treatment towards him which was not a part of the usual process. Aurim could cut corners and skip certain parts of the rituals since he caught on to the lesson faster than the others. This was a grave error on the part of these noblemen. The problem was that they had been initiating Rahsan for so long that they grew bored with the tedious methods. They had forgotten the instructions of their teachers and the deeper meaning of some of the more cosmic sub-rosa inculcated within the teachings. Salamander paused and said "a fence missing one board, isn't a fence at all"

He took another sip of his drink and then continued the history lesson. These lazy Noblemen caused a chain reaction that reverberated across all the realms in existence. They had accidentally let a child of Hsub gain access to the secrets of the Rahsan people. Although it was not a clear threat at first. But as the training progressed it became clear something was not right about this young man. He was always very jealous of the others. Even though his skin was the darkest brown the other kids' skin was much darker. He always felt he was different, and that he always had to be better than the others even though he was favored by the noblemen. Aurim was quick to tell a lie to get the young Rahsan girls to pay attention to him. in sparing exercise Aurim would tend to be too aggressive with the others. The noblemen shrug it off as misguided adolescent energy and figured he would grow out of it. The days turned into weeks, then months and finally years of training had passed and now the initiation was complete.

It was time for the new brothers to meet the High Noble Priest of the Society. At the time This was your grandfather who was known as "Grand Master TeeTee"

The young men were led to a circle deep in the jungle with a stone alter that rose from the ground with the secret book of Rahsan wisdom on top of it. John abruptly shouted out with excitement I have been there! Salamander smiled and said yes, you have been there, and just like these young men you were initiated into the priesthood. However, the methods have changed. These young brothers went through the physical part of the training and learned the secrets before taking the oath. We realize now that this was a mistake, so now we allow the pupils to choose the path first before any of the mysteries are conferred.

There are grave penalties for breaking the secret oath. however, if one knows the mysteries they can be passed on to the wrong people before anyone would be alerted and so is the case of Aurim. Salamander's face was full of disappointment as he described the next invents that would lead to my Grandfather TeeTee and my father Mungu's capture.

Unbeknownst to the Noblemen who had trained Aurim, he had been contemplating his position in the community and dislike of the other kids. He thought "why am I so different than the others?" he thought about all the subtle differences between him and everyone else. His attitude towards the knowledge he was given. the other kids liked the lessons but for him, it was like he had been deprived of them, and learning the secrets felt like he was only taking something that belonged to him. he figured there had to be a reason. this was not an accident of nature. Aurim had the sinking feeling he was not being told the whole truth

Every day the question of who he was tore at Aurim's consciousness, it kept him up at night. His growing resentment for his friend and his harem mothers became almost unbearable. Until one day he asked one of his harem mothers who claimed to have given birth to Aurim, the most important question he could ever have asked. he went to his mother and said "mother I know I'm not your child. Please do not lie to me, who am I? Aurim's mother confuse and frozen in fear blurted out "you were found riding on a camel by a warrior shaman he brought you to us to love and raise. we have done so. Aurim stunned by the blunt admission leaned to the side and stumbled into a nearby chair. Aurim Silent for a moment sat in deep focus. Then he looked up at his surrogate mother with contempt and said if you know of any other information you had better release it at once. The harem mother was filled with horror and trepidation Aurim's voice had changed it was dark, raspy, and threatening the harem mother backed up toward a wall opposite Aurim said "there aren't but a hand full of villages around here" she continued almost sobbing "whoever placed you on that camel must have come from one of those!" then she fell to her knees crying, she had raised Aurim since and infant with all her heart she did not realize that he would someday threaten her like that. Aurim jumped up and went to the place where the village kept its maps. He found only two villages which he could have made that trip from. He did not even pack any clothing or food he just started walking out of town to find his real family.

Once the harem mother saw that Aurim was indeed gone, and it was safe to come out of the home she sent word to me. She told me in great detail what had happened but by the time I had received the message, it was too late Aurim had found his Birth mother and heard the whole story of not only his father's death but the history of Hsub and the Nashar people. Aurim told his mother that he would return to Dhahabu and finish his training, but he would first seek out his grandfather. Caliana begged him not to do so. She knew that Aurim had no idea of the hatred the Nashar had for the Rahsan and even though he was part Nashar they would show no mercy. Aurim then looked up into his mother's eyes and feeling sorry for her agreed to not look for his grandfather and return to Dhahabu. He spent a week with his mother and her friends and new family until it was time to head back. Aurim hugged them all and kissed his mother on the cheek promising to return to visit. He picked up a traveling bag Caliana had prepared for him and walked out the door. He walked a few feet turned and looked back. he smiled and waved goodbye when he turned back his smile faded into a scowl. He had lied, he was going directly to Egypt to see his grandfather. He would tell him all about the Rahsan and their secrets.

✹ ✹ ✹

Part 3

Aurim

The desert was searing as the Sun's flames beamed down licking the shoulders of Aurim causing more pain than usual. The sand dunes weaved into abstract designs that lined the trails made by the caravan of travelers Headed from west to east and then back again. Aurim had to switch tactics as the sun had become even more violent as the days went by. Aurim decided to make camp during the day and travel at night, so that sun could not attack him by Pilfering patches of his skin. He began to hide from the sun making small huts just before sunrise to completely cover himself and for weeks, he did not see the sun. Salamander paused then said, I believe this triggered the next events. He continued with the story. Saying, after about two weeks of hiding from the sun he began to show physical changes. he noticed his skin became much lighter with each day and that he grew to despise heat. By the time Aurim had made it to Egypt, he was completely colorless. The night he reached the entrance of the great city that had now been taken over by the Nashar he was greeted by the Guards "halt, who dares to enter our lands?!" Aurim replied hesitantly it is I Prince Aurim of the Hsub clan of the Nashar Nation. This was met with contemptuous guffawing that instantly stung Aurim. His temper began to swell like an uncontrollable fire in the pit of his stomach. Aurim growled and raised his hands cupping them and picturing the guard's throats in his grasp. the guards froze. the laughter that had flowed uncontrollably was abruptly cut short and replaced with gurgling noises. Their eyes bulging out of the bloodless pale faces released streams of tears as they faded into unconsciousness. Before they could completely pass out Aurim let them go. They both fell to the ground gasping for air. One of the guards was able to yell "Open the gates" before falling out from the lack of oxygen. There was a loud clang and clunk from behind the gates, then they slowly parted open from the middle. Aurim smirked, and walked toward the opening, stepping on the back of the guard who had fallen out. Aurim stepped proudly into the city surveying the land and its people. They looked like him for the most part. he had noticed that some of the citizens were not Nashar and serve as merchants and other workers. as Aurim made his way up the main road that led to the palace people stopped and took notice they smiled and waved politely as if they recognized him. a young woman who was clearly Nashar stared at Aurim. He could feel her glare. he focused on her and then he heard her speak without her making an audible sound. She said, "who are you, I have never seen you here?" to which Aurim replied, "I'm Aurim the grandson of Hsub."

The main road to the castle was made of golden n bricks. that sparkled like stars in the moon's light creating an exact replica of the night's sky. As Aurim stepped cautiously toward the Palace and his destiny he thought of the greeting he would receive. he imagen a great celebration at his return. Maybe his grandfather would throw a parade for him. Aurim grinned at the prospect of being honored in such fashion. Aurim came to the edge of the road where it began to ascend upwards to the palace to the right there was a carriage powered by four camels decorated with gold harnesses and fine silks flowing and florescent adorned with flowers and brass bells. The driver was an odd-looking man with stern elderly facial features that did not seem to match his muscular physique. He turned his turban-covered head toward Aurim his body stuck in the forward position. He asked "Hal Targhab fi altaseid?" which meant "do you wish to escalate" in Arabic. "Arabic was spoken by the lowers class citizens in the area. The Nashar adopted the language in public communication but used telekinesis to speak to one another." Salamander explained to the guys before continuing with the story. Aurim boarded the middle chamber of the carriage "yah" was shouted by the driver and with a snap of the silk ropes attached to the camels, the carriage moved forward the ride was smooth like being carried in the arms of an overprotective mother. the carriage swayed gently from side to side. There was gold incent holders at the four corners of the middle chamber from which light smoke launched. creating an intoxicating scent in the air as the warm breeze swam in and out of the chamber's open windows looking out the side, Aurim could see the lower lands sink as he rose closer to the palace. He was home so he thought. The amazing ride into the heavens took a while. as the sun began to make its way into the sky, light began to wrestle Darkness into submission. Aurim frowned as he saw his new enemy rise as he was rising. Aurim wrapped his scarf around his face covering his nose and mouth leaving only his eyes unprotected. After a while longer the caressing sway of the carriage came to a gentle stop and the driver climbed down from his perch and slightly bowing, he opened the door motioning to Aurim to exit. Which he did with excitement. Aurim leaped down to the golden floor in the courtyard he stared up at the large white palace each of the 8 towers that lined the walls of the structure was capped with large domes made of diamonds. The walls of the palace were blemish-free and not a speck of dirt could be found anywhere. Aurim started to walk to the front door when he noticed that he was so high up that he could see the pyramids he instantly wondered why his grandfather had not chosen to live there, this palace was beautiful but still paled in comparison to the great pyramids with their glowing white walls of pure Marble that reflected the brightness of the sun. Aurim made a mental note to ask his grandfather about this decision He approached the big red door there were guards flanked on both sides. Dressed in all Black their faces were covered with gold masks. One of them spoke out, "who come here?" the abruptness of his voice startled Aurim. But Aurim quickly regain his confidence and shouted back "it is Aurim Son of Suseg and grandson of Hsub!" the guards did not move. the warm wind blew through their garments causing a series of waves over the tall frames. A long uncomfortable silence was broken by the camel's grunts and stumbles. They could sense the tension in the air. Then one of the guards spoke to Aurim with his mind. He said, "your father was a trader to his people, and you are the result of this crime, we have every right to kill you, where you stand" he continued "by what right do you seek audience with the great Hsub?" Aurim now frightened tried desperately to find an answer that would save his life and get him a chance to speak with his grandfather. Aurim replied send word to my grandfather that I have been taught the secrets of the Rahsan and I can help find the new lands they occupy. The guards looked at one another and then quickly opened the big red door and one by one squeezed through the opening. Aurim waiting for hours, the sun had risen to its zenith.

the Sun's rays beat down on Aurim viciously and even though he had his clothing covering every part of his body the sun still punished him. Suddenly the door opened and one of the guards beckoned to Aurim, he jumped up from under one of the camels where he had been trying to hide from the sun and ran full speed to the door. As Aurim slid inside he felt a change in the climate instantly as his eyes widen at the scene inside the palace. "All ice, Aurim whispered to himself" as he removed the scarf from around his face feeling the ice-cold air that caressed his cheeks. He could feel the icy floor on his feet healing the damage done by the hot sands of the desert he crossed. Aurim notice that no one was wearing a lot of clothing and so he stripped down to his pants and thin under-shirt. He basked in the frigid palace. He smiled from ear to ear. The colder it got the better he felt. He now knew what it was like to be home he was Nashar. but now he had to make his grandfather understand that he was committed to his Nashar heritage and despised the Rahsan blood that existed within him. the was a large staircase leading up to a grand floor the guards ushered Aurim up them quickly and into the main room where the overseers met to discuss important matters. Aurim was guided to a seating place in front of a long U-shaped table. The guard made a sign with their hands and slowly backed out of the room closing the door behind them. The room was made of Ice the chandeliers that hung from the ceiling were large ice cycles of light on every wall there were pictures of people pure white colorless in appearance. Some were dressed as warriors and others as some sort of statesmen and women. One picture had a black curtain over it. Aurim wondered who that could be. Just then people began to enter through a door from the chamber at the back of the large room. They made no eye contact with Aurim. He again became Nervous. As the people filed in alternately going to the right and then left side of the table until all the seats had been taken up except for the large thrown that sat in the middle of the U-shaped table. A servant girl who was visibly freezing in the iceberg of a room came to place an ice cube in Aurim's left hand and said, "Squeeze this" and so Aurim grasped the cube tightly. The servant girl turned and hurried away. There was a moment of silence and then one of the people at the table said, "Hold out your hand and show us the ice!" so Aurim stood up and held his hand out. He opened his palm, and the Ice was still there with only and bit of melting. A single drop fell turning to ice before it made its way to the floor shattering into pieces. The people at the table turned to each other they were communicating telepathically but Aurim could not hear them this alarmed Aurim. Another one of the people at the table stood up and said aloud "you have the blood of the enemy flowing through your veins, however, the Nashar blood had all but taken over your cells, this is an interesting ordeal you are no doubt one of us." Just then another person stood to speak, "you must learn the history, before you can go any further" then each of the people stood and told a part of the history of the Banished Ones and the great savior who came and saved them. After hearing the cruel treatment of his people Aurim was sure he was doing the right thing. He felt pride in his grandfather and how he was able to fight back and free his people. Aurim could feel his heart turn to ice as the rest of his blood cells were now transformed, he was no longer part of Rahsan, he was now All Nashar. "Hold out your hand, show us the ice!" one Nashar said. Aurim raised his hand and the ice had frozen completely there were no drops.

The Nashar at the table had not only given the history they had been performing a sacred ritual that turned Aurim completely. The ritual was now finished and the large door to the chamber opened again. In walked a tall thin man with glowing blueish white skin it reminded Aurim of an arctic glacier's hue. All the Nashar rose and place their hand forward with their palms up. And spoke in unison telepathically but this time Aurim could hear clearly "Hail Hsub, lord of the multi-Realms known and unknown" this was repeated three times until they all were signaled to sit. The man took his seat on the throne, not yet making eye contact with Aurim. He asked, "have the previsions been made?" to which one the Nashar answers "Yes! Lord, the transformation is complete." Just then the man's eye darted up towards Aurim. He spoke "I am Hsub, Lord Wizard King of the multi-realms those known and unknown. I exist everywhere that there is thought and everywhere thought will be." He continued; we the Nashar people were once considered the lowest form of existence but now we are the highest of all. Through war, we have taken control as to bring forth a new reality. We have driven the Rahsan out of most of the realms and now we are on the move to completely wipe them out for good. Once this is done, we can get rid of this retched Sun who hurt us so. That my child is the ultimate goal for our people." Then Hsub lead forward and whispered, "Is that your goal too...grandson?" Aurim now teeming with pride leaped to his feet and shouted, "if it's the last thing I do." Hsub leaned back on his throne rubbing his icy cold hands together he replied with a sinister grin "Good."

Hsub paused then said "Now tell Me everything"

And Aurim Began to tell all he knew about the Rahsan people their rituals and secret languages and method of finding other worlds and realms. For days Aurim was asked about plots and plans. And Aurim day in and day out willingly gave up all he knew. There were times when Hsub would summon Aurim, and they would go for walks around the palace. Hsub would show Aurim Painting of family members and Scenes of great Battles. Aurim felt comfortable with giving up all his knowledge for a deep sense of belonging. Fortunately for the Rahsan Aurim only knew the secrets up to a certain level. Since he had left before being told the last key, he was not an actual master but sort of a master's apprentice. Therefore, he could not give all of the Secrets. Salamander paused and grinned to himself as he told John and the crew. "This was my idea to break up the lessons into levels or degrees, this way there was not a chance of anyone getting to the great and holy Secret without being detected by those who possess it. Each level you obtain changes you, if you do not change then there is something wrong and your mind must be erased and the levels you had learned would be removed." John said "man all of this is just too much to bear. I'm not sure I can handle the funk that comes with this shit." Salamander grabbing his glass said before taking a long sip "shiiiiiit, little nigga you in the shit now, and ain't no turning back fa' none of ya'...You dig?"

The crew all nodded in the affirmative. "Now listen up, there is more to the story" Salamander began again. "It was days and days of information given to the Nashar. on the seventh day, Hsub summoned Aurim into his chambers. Once Aurim arrived Hsub had Aurim have a seat on his throne. When Aurim was nice comfortable Hsub asked Aurim "how does the throne feel? "wonderful" Aurim replied getting even more relaxed as Hsub crept to the back of the throne. pointing his long pale finger out towards a large window on the left wall of the large room, Hsub said "imagen having control over millions of Nashar from this throne, placing fear in the hearts and minds of whoever you come across, causing doubt where there was once confidence. Destroying hope for all the little Rahsan children. Terrorizing and oppressing them until the thought of rebellion does not even cross their tiny minds." Until they hate their position in our reality so much, that they begin to hate and even kill each other!" "How does that sound Aurim?" Hsub asked gently. "How does taking over this reality sound? Do you think you can handle the unlimited power? Aurim answered, "yes, Grandfather." Aurim continued "I could handle all of that and much more"

Hsub's grin slowly melted away. As he kneeled and slightly poked his head around the left side of the throne showing his Menacing face and said "your father said the same thing" before Aurim could reply his voice was cut short by the warm blade that slashed swiftly across his throat held by the little servant girl. Aurim grabbed his neck trying feverishly to hold the blood that gushed from his wound he managed to stand before falling face down on the long U shape table. his blood freezing as it flowed over and dripped onto the floor. "God Dam!" Jamal shouted shaking his head back and forth. "Hsub killed his own grandson, why?" he asked.

Hsub, does not know how the change Rahsan into Nashar or vice versa. If this were true, he would have never waged this war. He always planned to kill Aurim. he was Half Rahsan and would always be. Once he got all the information, he could get from Aurim he became useless and therefore had to be dealt with, and so the story goes. Aurim is Dead at the hands of his own grandfather.

VIII

Chapter 8

We form like Voltron!

John, Jamal, Dame, Ed, and Uncle Sonny just stared in silence their thoughts racing. Dame then said, "if this dude would kill his own Grandson, just what the fuck would do to us?" "Dam right" Sonny exclaimed. "Look man, I can dig the history lesson about the wizard and warlocks' shit, but you talking about some serious evil mutha fucka, who is tracking us down to annihilate us all and we are talking about going to find his ass? Shiiiiiiiiid" sonny said while shaking his head in disagreement. John who was still silent stood up and walked to the front door turning and placing his back against it he spoke to the crew. "Death is not real; we are no longer blinded by the false reality of this simulated world. We now know better, so we must do better." He continued "look, guys, Salamander saved me from the dope, and now I must repay him. and on top of that I now know my father and grandfather are alive and somewhere suffering, I must do something." John dropped his head and said in a tone regretful tone "even if I have to go it alone"

The crew looked around at each other and right there it was decided that they all would go on the journey together.

Salamander leaped to his feet and shouted then it's settled grinning from ear to ear his gold teeth shimmering. The first thing we must do is find ourselves an army. "How do we do that?" asked John. Salamander quickly responded "whelped for starters there are a bunch of Rahsan who do not know they are Rahsan right here in North Oakland there is a great concentration of them up in the Bushrod Park Area. We will go up there and speak with a Chief named Scooty D, he knows all the people in the area, and he can help us gather them for training. Be warned most of our people have been affected by Racism, drugs, and alcohol so we will have to give them the special dope to get them clean first."

The brothers walked outside to the front yard where Salamander's car was waiting. "We can't all fit in that car, dude," Jamal said disappointed. Then Sonny said, "some of us can ride in my car!" the brother just looked at each. Nobody wanted to ride in sonny's car because it was an old beat-up Cadillac Seville. Filled with dents and scrapes. The paint had faded drastically on the hood and rooftop. The brothers grinned and snickered at the thought of having to ride with sonny.

Salamander tilted his hat to the left and walk over to sonny's car and placed his hands on the front headlight. Then he whispered some magical words that sounded like a rap song I had once heard. The car suddenly began to shake, and the dents started to straighten out. The scratches disappeared as the paint became bright and glossy. The tire's rubber became new, and the rims contorted into fresh star wires and vouge tires. The interior transformed into a peanut butter color bucket seat with matching dashboard and door panels everything trimmed in gold.

After salamander had finished making over the Seville, the brothers were fighting each other trying to get in the front seat. Sonny just stood there grinning from ear to ear, beaming with pride. He walked to the driver's side, opened the door, and slide into the seat. After adjusting the mirror and driver's seat to his liking he put the key in the ignition and turned it forward. The engine roared to life. Sonny reached for the golden knob that controlled the radio. Click! And the radio lit up releasing a sparkling clean wall of sound. The group was 'Whodini' the song "freaks come out at night" crystalized this moment in time, as something to never be forgotten. Sonny, Jamal, and Ed Roe rode together while John and Dame rode with Salamander.

They slowly rolled through the north Oakland streets like two multicolored reptiles looking for their next meal. They weave in and out of traffic. Attracted attention from all that saw and heard the carnival-like parade of magic vehicles crawling up the blocks. As sonny followed behind salamander's ride. He realized that they were riding all over the north from Apgar to Gaskill. From 45th to Roach Ville and then on to Bushrod.

They crept up Shattuck ave. until they hit 59th street. making a right the big wooden sign's letters which had originally been white were now colored in Red Black and Green they read Bushrod Park underneath a message was carved in the wood HOE OR DIE! could be seen by all who thought about trespassing on the turf.

As the two cars rolled up 59th the curtains in the large front windows that lined the right side of the street opened and closed all the while young members of the Bushrod rod parks army arouse from back yards marching to the parks parking lot Salamander followed by Sonny eased into the lot and found two spots. Instantly the young soldiers began to crowd the lot some holding large guns at their waist. These young brothers beamed with pride and attitude to match. They wanted to see who had the balls to pull up their turf especially unannounced that type of stuff just did not happen over here.

Salamander exited his ride, displaying his gold tooth smile. This disarmed the youngsters they were tripping off Salamander's clothes although they were funny looking to them it made them feel that he was some kind of important cat. They backed off a bit, allowing an older youngster to make his way to the front. He was a tall kid with a slender but muscular build, he sported a short "baby Jesus" style perm.

He was sizing Salamander up, looking him up and down. But salamander being a seasoned wizard and master of Rahsan culture quickly communicated to the young bull his strength without opening his mouth. The youngster displayed his own brand of power by yelling "Bushrod High!" to which the large crowd of young girls replied "HOE OR DIE" this was done three times until a pathway was made that led from the parking lot to the baseball field and into the dugout area.

There Stood a group of Black men known as the council

of elders on this turf as well as the immediate area these brothers almost matched Salamander's flair for style They wore gold rings and medallions as big as the sun. they seemed to shimmer as they passed large joints of Marijuana back and forth. All of them wore different patterned outfits but they all had the same red, black, and Green Motif. The dug was lined on both sides with white linin. council members sat in chairs with space for visitors in the middle. at the back of the small space sat 'Chief Scooty D' he wore a long Dashiki that went down to just above his ankle. his hands and wrist were covered in gold and diamonds rings and bracelets the top of his head was a high-top fade that rose to the sky this was a Rahsan hairstyle reminiscent of a true Rahsan king of the past. His mouth was full of gold teeth and when he spoke the sun's light would jump from tooth to tooth reflecting its shine on his every word. He held a gigantic perfectly hard-wrapped cigar filled with the best Marijuana herbs around between his two fingers as he held court. Once Salamander reached the council's makeshift chambers. The council members all turned to see him at the entrance the only thing that moved was the smoke from the many joints lit. Through the thick smoke, Salamander could be seen standing. With great confidence and Showmanship, he allowed the moment to sink in and after he was satisfied with his effectiveness he bowed slightly and greeted the chief. He said, "U Hali Gani?" which meant "how are you" in Swahili. The chief stared intensely as the smoke from his cigar danced around the space. Like a silver ballet dancer twisting and turning into the Either. Then he replied "Sijambo" which means "I'm fine"

The chief then grinned. He was amused by the attire

Salamander wore. He sensed something familiar about his new guest. The chief extended his marijuana cigar to Salamander which Salamander received gladly. Taking a long pull of the strong herb into his lungs holding it for a few seconds and then slowly releasing the thick smoke from his nose and mouth. YES, YES, YES! Salamander spoke joyfully acknowledging that the chief had some exceptionally good Herbs.

The chief was delighted and asked Salamander "to what do I owe the pleasure of you visit my brother?" "Well, kind sir" salamander explained. "The information I am about to share with you will change your understanding of who and what you and your family and friends are." The chief leaned forward to get a clearer look at his guest. "Go on" the chief whispered.

And Salamander removed his coat and swirled his hands around making and design in the air that soon became streams of lights. Once everyone in the makeshift hut slash palace had become focused on the light...He took them.

Everyone had disappeared for 5 seconds but all those outside of the tent Had not noticed a thing. Then they reappeared as if nothing happened except for the people and chief being clearly shaken by the experience. Little Jesse the chief's cousin yells "hey man what the fuck was that? Where were we?" Salamander quickly replied "that was the land of your ancestors. That was a quick rundown of your history. you are all Rahsan people." he explained "you are a part of an ancient powerful people who have been dispersed throughout different realms, time, and space. We are now being tracked by our enemies and we must come together to fight and forever rid our minds of this scarce." The chief stood and said

"Mr. Salamander, you have our full support. Then he shouted, "Bushrod high!" to which the whole neighborhood replied, "hoe or die!" this could be heard as far away as Emeryville and the Oakland hills which were half a mile away in each direction.

Salamander thanked the chief and then told him that their first mission was to clean up all the known Rahsan people and free them from the drugs that plagued the community. Salamander made a circular motion with his hands and a big bag appeared in his palms. He gave the bag to a high-ranking member of the council who was an expert electrician and energy worker named E-Moseby, but he was known as Black superman around North Oakland. E, examined the contents of the bag and "asked what this is?" It is a special kind of herb made into a concentrate that will eliminate all the impurities out of a junkie's body. It will make his or her system as well as their minds brand new. We must put this out on the street, and once our people are clean then we can form our army and go on the attack! can you dig it? Salamander asked. "Yeah, yep I can dig it shu' Nuff" Black Superman answered.

Salamander swung his coat's long cape as he turned towards the exit of the hut slash palace and walked out. The crew was still waiting by the cars by this time they form a semi-circle and they were taking turns freestyling with the younger Park Boys. Salamander stood listening till John had finished his rhymes, and then he motioned to the crew to get in the cars. The roar of Salamander's vehicle rumbled the eardrum of all within the parking lot, as the heavy bassline of Parliament Funkadelic's Atomic dog filled the atmosphere with the deep synth and hypnotizing funk. Both cars slide slowly out of the parking lot and up 59th street as George Clinton sang "why must I be like that, why must I chase the cat" sinking into the distance. All the park boys grew smaller in salamander's rearview mirror as they headed to the next turf.

☀ ☀ ☀

IX

Chapter 9

BUSTIN' OUT, OF THE L7

Salamander along with John and the rest of the crew hit every turf in North Oakland. There were the 6-1 sland boys, The Apgar click, 5-6, The Gaskill crew, Roach Ville, and the Herzog gang. And with a little encouragement, they all agree that no drugs would be sold in or around those hoods and at the same time, they would administer the super dope to clean up all the junkies in the north.

But there was one big problem, the major supplier of drug the dope that was poisoning our streets for decades was coming from a big-time organization who at its core was run covertly by the government and by the evil Nashars. They would have to fight to clean up the streets and keep them clean.

After a long day of politicking with the people, the crew returned to the pink house on 61st and MLK. The crew was immensely proud of themselves they laughed and gave each other dap. Then salamander turned to John and beckoned him forth. All the guys fell silent as salamander began to twist his hands as he had done before, a light grew in his palm, and a flash of light burst, and a black hat reminiscent of a godfather gangster hat, but the brim was shaped like a base caps brim. A bright red band hugs the base of the headpiece and a long feather sticks out from it. John stood there looking at the peculiar hat wondering who it was for. Salamander presented the headdress to John and told him that every great wizard has his own hat. At first, John was tempted to refuse the strange cap but something about the design called to him John reached out took the hat, and placed it gently on his head John instantly felt a tingle down his spine as if the hat was connecting to his mind and body. a slight glow covered John as he adjusted the brim to sit at an ace deuce tilt to the left side of his head. John turned to the others and asked, "how does it look?" to which Ed roe quickly replied "hella clean!" ed roe looked over at the salamander and asked, "do I get one?" Salamander grinned wide and answered, "why of course you are all Rahsan wizards, and you will now rock the dress code of such." Just then Salamander waved his hands, and three other hats appear on the dining room table. Sonny, Jamal, and ed roe walked over to the table and each pick the hat that best complemented their style and attitude. Salamander smiled and said "Exodus 4:12, I will be with thy mouth, and teach thee what thou shalt say... Let us begin." Salamander spent the next 7 days Teaching the crew Magic Spells and conjuring tactics. The crew learned about Rahsan warriors who fought in this realm against the soldiers of the Nashar like Francois Mackendal who led revolts in Haiti. Some call him a voodoo priest but the Rahsan know the magic he used was very ancient. Salamander spoke of great women like Cécile fatiman who was able to conjure the great spirit that helped Bois Caiman fight against the Oppressors who were under the control of the Nashar. He talked about the Universal subconscious mind that binds us all and the connection between personal grooming and sorcery. He said, every hair is an antenna, and it must be kept clean and situated in the proper style to receive righteous vibrations from Nature. this will keep you strong and help you attract the right people and material objects into your life. He taught them how certain colors, bring out emotions in people before you even say a word. He also taught them about fragrances that ward off evil. Most importantly he took them to the back yard where they practice hand-to-hand combat. this would come in handy when it was time to go to the other realm and fight the Nashar. on the 7th day, they rested and reflected on the teachings and how the ancient ones lived their lives in conjunction with the great San, which we now call the sun. how meditation helps them communicate with everything around them. The trees, animals, insects, and other people. Even the wind is a friend of the Rahsan.

John loved hearing the stories of the old times and could not wait to go to the other realms. He was proud of himself he was more than just some junkie stumbling around the city in a technicolored nightmare. He was a Rahsan.

It was high noon in the city of Oakland and John wanted to take a drive to check out the spots to see if there had been any resistance to the new plan as well as to check out the east and west to create a citywide alliance against the destruction of all the people. But first, he would have to stop by the mall to pick out some new garments to match his Wizard's hat. John took the dress code profoundly seriously.

He picked up the key to sonny's car and headed for the door. Salamander watched his eyes follow John and before John could twist the doorknob Salamander shouted, "say jack, how are you gonna just take another man's ride like that?" John startled by the question, stuttered "I, I was about to go for a drive maybe pick up some clothes and check our traps" Salamander then exploded with laughter. Then he took a deep pull from the joint he had been holding. The ends fiery glow brightens and crackled. He exhaled a white cloud of smoke and said, "Hey baby it's all good, but you need your own ride to style and profile in, ya' dig?" Salamander paused and then continued. he asked John in a deep southern drawl. "Say, my man what kinda load you like? deuce and a quarter or let me guess, Cadillac Coupe Deville? He then chuckled to himself as he stood up and did a little shimmy with his shoulder. He said, "The ways of the Mack are meticulous and arduously complex." He continued "you cannot just be any geek off the street. Everything must be in line with your natural self your vehicle must be unique and representative of your own vision. Once again, your ride should speak before you do. Ya' feel me, baby bubba?!" John thought long before he answered. Then he said excitingly "Shiiiid, man, I know what I want, a mutha fuckin' 68' ford falcon two-tone red and white with red interior. John thought about his father's old car that had been kept in storage since his capture by the Nashar. John and the crew all rode over to John's house on 56th and went to the back yard of the old beat-up shed where the Falcon was kept. John lifted the front door a wall of dust and dirt spilled into the air causing them to cover their faces to escape the particles John coughed and fanned away the dusty cloud. It was dark and stinky the falcon was covered by an old blanket with African Kinte print. Sitting around the shed were hundreds of books and note pads. Jamal reached down and picked one up. As he thumbed through it, he saw cartoon illustrations of different black characters all in action poses the detail in these drawings were mesmerizing, Jamal could not put the artwork down. He read the name signed at the bottom and recognized it immediately it was Mungu's he was the illustrator of the artwork. Jamal who was quite the artist as well asked John if he could take the artbook home. Jamal felt that something was compelling him to study the drawings and he wanted to do just that. John nodded in the affirmative. So, Jamal tucked the art book under his arm and continued to move the other books away from the Falcon.

Once all the books were moved John grab the bottom of the blanket and slowly folded it backward revealing the front end of the falcon. He continued to fold the cover until the entire car was visible. Salamander opened the driver side door and got in he flipped the sun visor down the keys that had been hidden there fell into his lap, finding the ignition key he inserted it into the switch and turned it forward to unlock the gears he pulled the gear shift downward the white line on the gear panel jumped to the letter D placing the car in drive position then the rest of the crew got behind the car and pushed. At first, the falcon would not budge but salamander added a little magic by snapping his fingers and making a rolling signal with his index right hand. The falcon began to give way and rolled slowly out of the dark and dirty shed into the sun's bright light.

The guys were amazed at the condition the falcon was in. no deep dents, just some scratches, and minor bumps. It needed a new paint job and chrome pieces replaced along with a vinyl top but other than that the falcon was well preserved.

Salamander, climb out of the driver's side and danced half-way down the driveway, and turned. He lit a freshly rolled joint. Moved close to the side of the house and leaned against it tipping his hat forward to cover his eyes he said "Now...you niggas get busy." As he blows out the marijuana smoke toward the crew. Everyone was confused, they had no tools or equipment to even wash the falcon let alone fix any engine problems. Then Dame spoke up "hey dude how the fuck are we supposed to get busy (making air quotes with his fingers) with no dam tools to GET BUSY (repeating the air quotes) with huh?"

Salamander just shook his head in disgust, "you little ugly ass mutha fuckas, make me want to regurgitate" he continued "we just spent a whole goddam week practicin' the ancient art of wizardry and you bumpkins are asking me about some jive-ass tools? for shame! I tell you... for... God...Dam... Shizzame"

Sonnie grasping what was going on turned to the car and began to focus on the chrome grill he stared with great focus, as salamander began to grin. he whispers "yes, that's it Sonnie show these young punks what time it, tiz." the more Sonnie focused on the chrome the more a slight breeze grew, and the more patches of dirt began to fall off until the entire grill was clean glisten in the sun. Sonnie then let out a sigh of relief, he had become worn out by the exertion of his power. The crew ran up to Sonnie congratulating him and celebrating what he had done. Then salamander stood straight up and turn his back on the crew he took a few steps toward the street and then stopped and while looking back over his left shoulder he said, "Okay gentlemen this is where I bid you adieu." The crew instantly got quiet they were shocked at what they heard. "What?!" Ed roe shouted out, "Ah-DO?" He questioned "say, man, if you gotta shit that's yo business, I gotta doo doo too but you do not hear me announcing it to the world!" to which dame replied, "he's saying he is leaving, dip shit" "oh okay, well dam" ed roe still confused then said, "Well why is he announcing he is leaving, to take a shit?!" John could no longer hold his laughter, he thought to himself, this nigga Ed roe always making shit funny. "QUIET! nimrods" salamander shouted in a serious tone. You niggas got ya'll instructions in Rahsan magic, use your powers to fix this car and get you some new treads, keep the drugs out of the ghetto and continue to build the army and when its time I will be back to lead you into the other realm. Now I expect some push-back from the local suppliers be ready. You could feel the tension in the air so much, so Jamal's stomach tightened up and he accidentally let out a long low tone fart that lasted 20 seconds. everybody slowly turned toward Jamal with inquisi-tive frowns. Jamal shrugged his should and whispered, "sorry ya'll I'm nervous." They all turned back to salamander but to their surprise, he had disappeared without a trace. The crew stunned for a moment quickly got their mind together. They knew it was time to use what they had learned from Salamander. First the car, then the clothes, and then the North. Each of the crew focused on a part of the car to restore John open the door and concentrated on the interior until it matched the image he held in his mind. Jamal asked, "what kind of tires should a falcon have?" "Why, Trues and vogues of course" Dame answered. Jamal waved his hands and got into a karate pose he had seen in the kung fu movies he saw at the lux theater. Suddenly the tired inflated and a white and thin yellow strip appeared around all the tires as the rims metamorphized into sparkling gold. Ed roe walked around the car adding and polishing all the chrome pieces. Once they all had finished, they all took a few steps back and admired their work. The 68' was brand new from the top to the tires. Sonnie walked over to John and held out his hand and said to John "Give me five." to which John quickly complied, slapping Sonny's hand making a loud clap.

"Right on, blood!" Sonnie whispered in a cool player's tone the crew fell silent and just stared at the 68'

☼ ☼ ☼

X

Chapter 10

THE PLAYER HATERS

After weeks of pushing the new drug, that cleaned the streets and detoxed the addicts. word got back to the low-level distributors just as Salamander had said. A phone call was made, and the voice explained "the North Oakland turfs were not buying any dope and that some dudes in funny hats had been preaching about cleaning up the streets." The call was received High in the Oakland Hills in a pristine mini-mansion. a large evil-looking man sitting at a long marble desk listening intensely to the voice on the other end nervously explains that there was no money to be turned in.

The Man's breathing become heavy as his disdain for this information became more intolerable. The Man then suddenly drove his huge fist down onto the marble desk, it crashed against the cold marble making a loud thud like Thor's hammer colliding into the earth. He screamed "I don't want to hear another word about what's not happening." he pauses trying to regain his composure. His next words were drenched in venom as he leaned forward in his throne-like chair, and said "listen to me very carefully you stupid mutha fucka, you and the rest of your buddies are up to your necks in this game, and that is exactly what will be cut, from ear to ear if you do not bring me this asshole in the funny hat; do you understand me?" the voice on the other end replied shakingly "y-y-yes sir, we're on it"

The Man leaned back in his oversized chair and contemplated his next move. His eyes darted back and forth in the sunken eye sockets of his round face flushed with red. he was genuinely concerned. he was just a middleman and soon the top bosses would be inquiring about the money that has all but dried up at this point. He ran his overweight fingers down his face wiping away the beads of sweat that continued to form. He then turned to an extremely well-dressed gentleman whose stature resembled a Zulu Chief from the old days. He stood to the right side just beyond the marble desk. the Man requested him to retrieve bottled water from the mini-fridge across the large home.

"Here you go Mr. Stanke'" the well-dressed man said as he handed the ice-cold beverage to his boss. Mr. Stanke' spun his chair around to face a large Window that extended from wall to wall. He slowly raised his 400lbs frame, standing to his feet. he walked over to the window and said to the well-dressed man "Wellington my friend... war is coming." To which Wellington nodded his head in confirmation and replied "I'm afraid so, Sir"

Charter me a flight to D.C. immediately Wellington we must go speak to the top guys.

The sounds of Too Short's "city of dope" blasted from the

speakers of John's falcon as he leaned far back in the seat, barely able to see above the steering wheel. His candy-coated magic sled was sliding slowly down Market St. like a majestic mechanism from the future, as he surveys the scene. the vibration from the deep bass melody, massaging his body. He thought to himself "it feels like the bass is going to rattle the car into pieces." John is laid back in the seat hypnotized by the groove. his eyes peeled analyzing the streets he can see the city changing into a healthier place to be as the fiends are introduced to the new dope. John pulls up on the corner of 45th and Market, where a bunch of kids is hanging out Infront of the liquor store. John rolled down the passenger side window and yells out "what is happening little brothers, what ya'll doing out here?" a sharply dressed youngster with a freshly faded high-top answered, "just waiting on some dummy to pull up and ask us a stupid question, but you here now so I guess we can leave!" the other kids burst out into laughter. John just grinned widely and yelled again this time with an insult "hey, little nigga...ya mama still on 48th selling booty for tube socks?" he continued "because I got a pair in my trunk" everybody on the corner including strangers walking by doubled over laughing. The young kid looked like he was about to cry. John quickly sensed he had gone a little too far and offered to make atonement. He said, "look man I'm just playing, I ain't even got no tube socks." John giggled to himself and said "here you guys come get some of this bread I got and buy yourselves some candy or something. All the kids on the corner rushed to the passenger side window to collect the money. After all the kids had received their money, John leaned over to the passenger side window making sure all the kids heard him "hey yall" he yelled "stay away from the fat man's dope and let me know if anybody who ain't from around the northside shows up pushing that bullshit, ya hear me?" yes! Screamed the kids in unison. John leaned back and quickly put the falcon into gear.

As the falcon leaped from the curb into traffic the tired squealed as thick white smoke streamed from the back tires creating a rubber-smelling cloud wafting down Market St. the Bass pounding like a giant stomping through the jungle. The kids froze at John's heroic departure into the interior of their ghetto dream staining their young subconscious memories.

John was headed to the west to speak with a childhood friend. a Mack named T-mail. He was known in the streets for being one of the biggest players around the entire bay area. He began in the north and migrated to the west and John figured he may be Rahsan. John needed allies in the other parts of the city in order to clean the streets and keep them within the righteous realm of the Rahsan people's nation. John eased down the road to 34th and market-making a right then he drove two blocks down and made a left on Chestnut St. "Westside Oakland!" John whispered proudly to himself. As John's falcon crawled slowly down the block to where a group of sharply dressed, tough-looking young men stood. He thought to himself "Bushrod is only fifteen minutes away from Chestnut, but worlds away in Aesthetics." "The north he continues to ponder was slick and glossy deeply rooted in a Players spirituality of sorts, but these niggas over here were different. Cutthroat hard-faced Hustlers, they did not play no games and bullshit will not be tolerated." John parked his ride and exited. "Say! what happenin' yall?" John asked loudly displaying as much confidence as possible. He wanted to make sure that the brothers understood he meant no ill will towards them, especially while on their turf. But John was met with silent stares. John began to rethink his mission. "shit" he thought. Realizing coming alone was not exactly a good idea he moved easily toward the group.

A voice came from a car parked in the driveway adjacent to the group of men. "that's far enough, brotha" the voice insisted. "What you want around here?" the voice asked. "Say baby I'm looking for a cat named T-mail, we go way back like a package with the wrong address, and I need to run down some heavy shit to the brotha, do you know where I can find him?" the tented window from where the voice escaped slid down completely revealing its owner. It was John's old friend T-mail. John grinned widely "what happening chump? t-mail said in a joking manner. John was super relieved and shot back "hey bustah, long time no see" John walked closer to the vehicle noticing the two extremely beautiful prostitutes that flanked T-mail, one stared laser-like into John's eyes while the other was powdering her nose with cocaine. John notice something about the two, their skin tone was odd. they were white women however their skin tone was unusually pale. John's stomach turned in disgust. ever since Salamander gave him the righteous dope, he was sickened at even the sight of any kind of narcotics. John turned his head slightly to lessen the effect of being around the cocaine. "Look man I got some wild shit to lay on you dude, and I need you to open yo' mind and hear me out," John explained. "I'm listenin'" T-mail quickly replied then continued "but first!" He said loud enough for the group of men standing outside to hear him "you gotta tell me, what's up with that weird ass hat, nigga?" T-mails eyes squinted tight as if he was listening with his pupils instead of his ears.

At that moment John sensed that T-mail was in fact Rahsan. He was searching for any kind of deceit in John's energy field or words. "This was why T-mail was at the top of the game, it was magic...Rahsan magic." John's excitement grew.

Then he began to tell the tale of the Rahsan and Salamander and the righteous dope. The People on 34th chestnut were captivated by the otherworldly yarn about Wizards and Magic, other realms as well as the great battle of 48th and Shattuck that took place recently.

T-mail was stuck after Hearing all of that. "Dam," he said in a muffled voice. John let him have a moment before dropping the bomb on him. John leaned in to the window, looked T-mail in the eyes, and told him. "My dear brother, you are Rahsan." And John continued "It is possible that everyone around you, is Rahsan as well." Just then one of the prostitutes yelled out angrily "sounds like a bunch of bullshit to me!" she turned to T-mail shouting "T you gone let this weird-ass mutha fucka come up on your turf and tell you some bullshit lies and fancy fairy tales, I thought you were a boss, shit you are slippin' sugar."

John paused; he was sensing the super negative energy arising from the two whores. John took a step back from the car. The whore's pupils both turned starch white. He realized at that moment that he was not the only one that had discovered T-mails Bloodline. The women were Nashar spies, sent to watch T-mail. John had to move quickly

Positioning his hand as if holding a small animal between

them. he then wiggled his fingers creating a small light that grew into a ball of energy. By this time, the two spies had burst from each side of the car. The door blew outward with a large boom. The crowd of tough guys ran for cover confused and afraid. The two spies were now standing directly in front of John. they had grown to ten feet tall and had a silver glow around their entire bodies. T-mail tried to exit the car but one of the spies waved her hand and he was thrown back into the back seat. the broken doors were then lifted and slammed back into place and smashed shut trapping T-mail.

T-mail yelled "what the fuck is going on, you demon bitches let me the fuck outta here!" the spy then flicked her hand causing the car to slide twenty feet away. While one spy was distracted with T-mail, John threw a blast of light at the other sending her flying backward and crashing through a large garage door, momentarily incapacitating her Seeing her sister injured the other spies turned to John and screamed shooting a dark beam of negative energy at John. But he quickly leaped high into the air just dodging the beam as it exploded causing a deep hole in the ground where he had stood. John then darted down like an eagle with great speed and focus ready to strike his prey but just as he was about to deliver his fatal strike the other spy woke up and in a split second countered John's attack with a disastrous blow to John's rib cage knocking him clear across the street into a parked car. The two spies sensing victory approached John slowly both displaying evil grins as they conjured up enough Energy to destroy John once and for all. They stood over John their eyes wide and bulging with rage one spy whispered "the Rahsan think they have the power to keep the Nashar from taking over the world and killing off the rest of your people? look at you your nothing but a junkie even if you manage to get some of your people off the dope they will come back once we kill you and your friends.

John stared up at the two women with surprise and fear. He thought "how could they know who I am, and about the plan?" just then one of the spies leaned down and whispered genteelly "aww look at him, he thinks he knows what this war is really about., silly fool" she exclaimed. "The Nashar are everywhere; we control this existence every world and every realm we are even inside your feeble little mind ever since the great lord Hsub liberated us." She chuckled and continued "oh yes and as soon as we find and destroy Willie Sharp, we will Rid the realms and all of existence of the Rahsan forever" the spies laughed John tried to remember where he had heard that name. then it hit him like a ton of bricks. He recalled what Salamander had said when they first met, "they used to call me Willie Sharp." As Salamander's voice echoes through John's head. The spies positioned themselves to strike.

but suddenly were startled by an explosion that came from behind them. they quickly turned to look and to their surprise, T-mail had broken himself out of the makeshift jail cell he was floating above the ground surrounded by a golden glow "step away from the pimpin,' you silly ass hoes" he commanded. John managed to pull himself up to his feet, and while the two spies had their backs turn John grabbed one of them by the neck and T-mail charged towards the other and a great battle ensued they fought from 34th chestnut down the block and around the corner to 32nd and linden St. Powerful punches, kicks, and Bright blasts of energy both positive and negative flew around the neighborhood you could hear the explosions for miles away for an hour. T-mail and John stood shoulder to shoulder breathing heavily from exhaustion. The Nashar Spies stood opposite of them also out of breath.

It was the final showdown. Then all of sudden a car appeared in the distance. The faint rhythm of funk music began to rise as the vehicle move slowly up the block. John began to giggle a smile smeared across his face. He reccgnized that car it was sonny and the crew coming to the rescue. The crew pulled up and as Parliament Funkadelic's flashlight provided the soundscape they exited the car like the Calvary coming to save the day!

Ed roe approach the spies and said "ain't you hoes supposed to be on some Corna,' getting some money." the spies seeing that they were surrounded decided to make an escape and live to fight another day "you chump, you couldn't send a letter to the post office, let alone send a bitch to the Corna to get money" one of the spies shouted at Ed Roe. Then they both shot a large beam downward creating a hole in the street into which they jumped and vanished. The Crew and T-mail just stare down into the hole relieved that the battle was over. But they knew they would have to fight them hoes again someday. T-mail, John and the crew agreed to meet up at E&J's Bar-b-que joint downtown Oakland. They needed to discuss the plans for cleaning up the streets in the west and how to move forward into the east. T-mail hopped in John's ride, as the crew loaded back up in Sonnies' and headed Downtown.

☀ ☀ ☀

XI

Chapter 11

WRONG ANSWER.

Meanwhile, on a private jet headed to Washington D.C. Wellington watches as Mr. Stanke sips on a Martini. His beady eyes darted from side to side like ping pong balls. while the hum from the jet's engines piercing the air at thirty-thousand feet created the soundtrack to his worry. Mr. Stanke's thoughts are fast and clear; he plans to let the top bosses know what is happening on the streets of Oakland. He needs permission to strike first. Or everything may be lost.

After five hours of flight, the bird landed at Dulles international airport where a long black limousine is waiting. a Tall burly gentleman with an icy cold stare greets Mr. Stanke and takes his bags to the trunk. Then the burly man rushes to the back door and opens it. "Here you are sir," said the burly man who was not only the driver but also the muscle in case of trouble. Wellington and Mr. Stanke both entered the limo and got comfortable.

The driver got into the car and slid the partition open

he asked in a raspy voice "would you like to go to the hotel or to the capital? The meeting is not for another 3 hours." Mr. Stanke annoyed by the question from the help said "just drive until I tell you to stop" then he laughed loudly, amused at his own humor. "Take me to my hotel, I have to shit if that's okay with you," Mr. Stanke said with a half-smirk on his round face.

The driver shut the partition and followed instructions. "Wellington my boy!" Mr. Stanke called out. "It looks like things are going to get pretty bumpy from here on out he continued "I'm going to need you to keep an eye out for any tomfoolery, I do not trust anyone at this point. We are just figments of the boss man's imagination, and we can be erased the moment we become useless; do you understand?" "Yes sir" wellington whispered.

The driver stared at wellington through the partition's transparent glass he thought that there was something very odd about Mr. Stanke's servant.

It was a forty-five-minute drive from the airport to the hotel. Once there Mr. Stanke and wellington entered the lobby while their bags were being unloaded as the concierge escorted them into the building. After checking into the swank five-star hotel it was up to the penthouse. The hotel was one of many front companies owned by the Nashar.

The penthouse was large and decorated in an ancient Roman style that highlighted the preposterous gluttony of Hsub's ideology. Bigger is simply better but opulence is religious.

There were gold statues of naked archers aiming their bows to the heavens to remind the viewer that man had his eyes on god's heaven and if God himself was not vigilant even he would fall to the Hsub's army. The large room was white, so white in fact it seemed to glow as the reflection of the sun pierced through the half-open curtains. There was a light wave of heat that permeated from the marble floor. As the two men stepped down into the large circular pit that contained a large round couch furnaced with bright colored pillows made of silk and satin a round crystal table sat in the middle of the pit held up by a golden calf sculpted to look as real as possible down to the veins in its skin. Large white vases supported bushels of red roses in each corner of the mini palace. A bar stocked with every expensive alcohol available was to the right of the pit. After getting comfortable Mr. Stanke ordered wellington to pour some libation to Cristian the new temporary home. "Pour up wellington my boy, let have a toast to this beautiful space we have for the time being and send a blessing up to the almighty that our business here goes as smooth as possible. Wellington grinned and nodded. then in a low agreeable tone, he uttered "yes sir, coming right up Boss." Wellington poured two glasses of 1980 Macallan 18-year-old sherry Oak single malt scotch. Wellington then delivered a glass to Mr. Stanke. The Ice cubes created a refreshing jingle as the cubes clank against the crystal glass like wind chimes on a summer day in the country. "Ahh, thanks, my Boy!" Mr. Stake said with glee. After swallowing his drinks in one greedy gulp Mr. stake propped his portly body up and took three short hops to get to his feet. Once up he shuffled to the toilet where once the door was secured loud grunts and flatulence escaped into the otherwise silent peace. Wellington laughed to himself as the fireworks continue from behind the bathroom door. "Goddam" wellington thought to himself "this mutha fucka is full of more shit than a Christmas turkey." Wellington scowled at the thought of what it must smell like in there. Shaking his head to escape the vile thought. Wellington finished the rest of his drink and headed to his room to unpack his bag.

After forty-five-minute Mr. Stanke came out of the cavern of all that be dammed release a horrid stench into the living area. Instantly wellingtons fear had been realized. The smell of death flooded the room causing wellington to choke. "Loud have mercy, boss." Wellington exclaimed, "an old beast must've eaten something that was dead, doused in spoiled milk, and then it crawled up yo' ass, waited for ten days took a shit, and then died." Mr. Stanke feeling a little embarrassed quickly replied. "Wellington, I pay to you for your service, not your opinion of how my shit smells, you hear me boy?" Wellington's smile dissipated quickly he understood the insult that was laced in the statement Mr. Stanke had thrown at him. calling a black man, "a boy" was like calling him a Nigger. Mr. Stanke grinned evil smeared across his pink face. The two stared at each other for a few minutes or so. The silence is broken up by the ring of the telephone. Mr. Stanke nodded his head toward the receiver motioning to wellington, who reluctantly walked over to answer it. "Stanke's residence," wellington said. He then nodded to Mr. Stanke alerting him, that it was the call from the big bosses. the voice on the other end gave instructions. the meeting was going to go down sooner than later and Mr. Stanke needed to start heading over to the meeting place quickly. "Yes sir" wellington spoke into the phone and then hung up. he then relayed the message to his boss. Mr. Stanke nervously gathered his coat and headed for the door walking passed the bathroom and quickly slamming the door after getting a whiff of his own ass. The two men headed downstairs and jumped into the limo, with the roar of the engine the chauffeur leaped into traffic headed to the meeting place.

Back in Oakland, the fellas had talked with Tyrone and devised a foolproof plan to distribute the righteous dope to the unconscious Rahsan people. Down in west Oakland, the brother's exchanged handshakes and dap. John bid T-Mail farewell. Not knowing that it would be the last time. The two-agent s of Hsub would come back and cast a deadly spell and T-mail would later be stricken with cancer and return to the eternal lands of our ancestry. A blow felt by all in Oakland.

Nightfall. as a pair of sleepy eyes peered up E14th. candy painted cars creeping by, blaring a myriad of slow-tempo rap and funk songs collectively creating a mesh of melodious heavy bass lows that Shook the concrete below John's feet.

"The Eastside" John thought to himself as he relinquished a cloud of Endo smoke from the large joint, he held. His eyes darted back and forth recording every site to be seen. John stood up straight un-Assing the sidewall of a church on the corner of 73rd Ave. The Neon sign of East Oakland Baptist church casts a heavenly glow down on his diamond-flooded neck, wrist, and fingers. As shadowy figures walked sheepishly past catching quick glimpses of the Black Prince. John was waiting on a cat he had reconnected with through T-mail. A slick-talking nigga named "Nairobi." Nairobi was known all over Oakland, but he was from a section called maxwell park. A lot of great Basketball players came out of that area. However, Nairobi was more than just a "hooper" he had family ties to the legendary

Black Panther Party for self-defense. Led by two Rahsan warriors Bobby Seale and Huey p newton. "Robi" as his friends called him was an expert barber as well, and the Warlord of a large nationwide motorcycle gang. John figured with Nairobi's influence and manpower he could help take over East Oakland and this would complete stage one of the plans. Again, John had a hunch that just like Tyrone, Nairobi was also a Rahsan Descendant. Just then the rumble of motorcycle engines in the distance began to claw at John's eardrum. The growling became increasingly intense. The synchronized slithering of multicolored bikes in and out of the wide lanes in between the traffic of E.14th St. was majestic and their helmets shined to perfection, sparkled in the night like flickering candles from a witch's seance in the dark woods.

Grandmaster Melle Mel's "Step off" charged from the speakers of Nairobi's cosmic shroom trip-colored bike as he reached the corner where John stood. John grinned, amused by the display as all the bikes began to pull up and back into a single row of bikes with their back wheels bouncing against the curb as they parked, all the riders facing the streets. This made for a quick getaway if shit got ugly.

After a quick moment of engine revving, the riders dismounted the iron horses reminiscent of outlaws of the old west. "John-boy is that you!" shouted Nairobi. "Is a pig pork, is midget short, is doctor J the king of the mutha fuckin' b-ball court?" John replied. As the two approached each other with large smiles. Their jovial greeting was accompanied by the sacred soul brother's handshake, complete with a twist, and turns of the wrist that was only learned and performed by the initiated few. "Shit nigga I ain't seen you in years." Said Nairobi. "And from the looks of thangs you done got clean." He continued "do my eyes deceive me or have the devil's hell gone colder than a whore ideal of fair deal?"

John leaned back spreading his colorful mink, displaying his diamond-studded belt bucket, and said "shiiiiid, nigga it doesn't take a telescope to see I've got my shit together baby bubba!" "I'm hip!" Nairobi said with pride. As he slaps his hands together, he said "So, let's get down to business good brotha." Nairobi's intuition was telling him he was about to be asked to get involved with something big.

"Right on" John replied, "here's the deal," John said as he began to run down the play. all the brothers from the gang gather around to hear the long tale. After about forty-five minutes Nairobi and his gang were speechless. it took a few minutes for the silence to be broken. Then a large brother moved in from the outer crowd. he was a heavy-set dude with a powerful aura. he wore red-framed glasses, and a large beard that sparkled from the afro sheen sprayed in it. The others parted like the red sea, spreading for Moses. When he got close enough to John, he extended his bear-like hands and introduced himself. "what's happenin' man, my name is bill" He continued I am second in command around here. I have heard your tale, and I for one am totally committed to the healing of our streets. So, if Nairobi says it is a go, I will personally take 10 kilos of the righteous dope and not only spread it around the deep east, but I will take it all the way to LA.

John Grinned and shook his head in agreement then he and bill looked at Nairobi. He gave the okay.

The deal was done and now it was time for some fun. Then Bill asked John "Hey man, why don't you join us up at the dragon's spot and let us celebrate the new partnership," John thought to himself for a moment and said "sure my man, I will dig you cats up there in a few" all the brothers came one by one to shake John's hand. He felt like a diplomat as they all mounted their iron horses and the sound of the engines coming to life in a thunderous wave once again vibrating the concrete under John's feet. John began to walk down the street giving an occasional head nod and peace to the rider as they blasted into traffic on their way to the EBD's clubhouse. John reached a phone booth and dropped a quarter into the phone thin slot. After dialing the number, the ringing tickle his eardrum until sonny answered "chello'" Sonny's voice came through in a melodic tone. "Say Unc. It's me John" he continued, "get the guys and meet me at the EBD's clubhouse in the deep we have been invited to a shin-diggaradoski!" John said laughing amused at his own joke.

"Okay sounds like fun, we will be there in about an hour, peace nephew"

John hangs up the receiver and turned carefully adjusting his mink and popping his collar. Grinning to himself he starts to strut to his ride.

The scene was electrifying. Motorcycles of all kinds lined both sides of E.14th street. there were hundreds of Black people gathered with one objective and that was to party and party as hard as humanly possible. there were cars from every era painted to grand perfection floating atop golden wire rims and white wall tires. You could hear the music of Too short, Mac mill, Freddy B, and MC Hammer pounding from

Kenwood stereo systems equalized by zapco boards and amps. Bright Neon pinks and green colored biker shorts hugged the thick curve of the women who paraded up and the block looking for a baller to seduce. Jheri-curls, 501's jeans, and white tee shirts were the uniform worn by the youngsters. Black with yellow striped Pittsburg pirate hats cock hard to the side signified their membership into the fraternity of sophisticated players raised in the home of the game. Big joints hung from the lips of the O.G.'s eyes red and low but still sparkling in the lime of the scene. John stood valiantly in the middle of this ballet of Black experience moving ritualistically. John's attire stuck out peculiar looks came from the youngsters but was admired by the older attendees. The elders were able to recognize the style. As John was digging the theater of soul, the fellas pulled up. Once they found a park, they all met up with John to enter the clubhouse. The sidewalk was tight and the walking room was thin at best. but the respect that the guy's attired commanded helped them navigate the sea of chocolate bodies.

Once they reached the front Bill was there to greet them and usher the guy into the club. The inside was even more intense than the outside. Thick Maryjane smoke filled the lungs of the brothers as Rick James's 'super freak' played as the soundtrack to the carnival of black colloquial conversations coming from all directions. It was a Magician's Paradise. The brothers were led to the VIP section where they were introduced to the leader of the EBDs Mr. T. Livingston. After the meet and greet was done it was time to party. The fellas copped a booth to be able to see the whole function they order bottles of champagne and cognac. John motioned to dame to roll up some of the righteous trees. Dame rolled up enough righteousness to get the whole California stoned. Then dame began to light each joint and pass them around to the people until almost every person had a joint in their hand. Then Jamal stood up and waved his hands slowly in a motion that gather the people's attention soon light began to form around Jamal and the brothers then it grew to encompass the whole room. Everyone started to notice that walls were waving to the rhythm of the music as the record slowed down and super freak morphed into Too shorts freaky tales. time and space were altered the whole room was being transported to the other realm. This was mass teleportation led by the brothers to party in the jungles of the mystic forest.

The party went on for what seemed like an eternity. While the others outside of the clubhouse had no idea of what was happening inside. Time and space are one and the same. As the beautiful people danced and reconnected with their true selves, they understood through mental telepathy that they all were Rahsan people and that it was time to reclaim their rightful place as peacekeepers and rulers of all existences under the Great San's blessing.

After the powerful drugs had taken effect and the Rahsan people had returned to their rightful minds. They felt clean and righteous, with clear views of their selves. They all rejoiced and thanked John and the crew. Oakland was back! Some yelled with complete joy.

☀ ☀ ☀

XII

Chapter 12

FUNK'N

Mr. Stake was meeting his Bosses. He was instructed to come to a large white home in a remote area of Maryland just outside of Washington D.C. about an hour away from the hotel. Once he and Wellington arrived, they were led through a large golden gate up a long driveway that came to a circle that turned back into itself leading back to the gate.

There was a butler at the entrance waiting for Mr. Stanke. when the car stopped, he reached for the door and beckoned Mr. Stake to exit. Then he snapped his fingers at which time a short pudgy man rushed to the side of Wellington and Mr. Stanke quickly took their coats as they walked up the large door of the home. Once in the house, there was an all-white lobby area and a noticeable temperature drop. Mr. Stanke looked at Wellington Nervously, as he rubbed his hands together blowing into his palms to heat them.

"Goddam it's kind of chilly in this mutha fucka don't you think?" Mr. Stank ask the butler. The Butler did not respond he just stared at Mr. Stanke and grinned devilishly. The butler turned slowly and whisper "this way please." he began to walk down a long hallway that went on for what seemed like four blocks. Mr. Stanke thought to himself. "The inside of the house didn't match the outside; this place was huge."

After walking for a while and observing the numerous painting and sculptures that lined the completely white hallway, they came to a double door with two awkwardly tall women standing guard at the front. the pudgy gentlemen quickly stumbled up to the woman and bowed down. the women nodded, and both reached for the handles opening on each side. the doors were obviously heavy as the women struggle slightly, pulling them apart. As Mr. Stanke and Wellington were then led into the large room. One of the large women stared at Wellington with a scowl as he passed by. It was like she could sense something she did not like about him. It made Wellington a bit Nervous, but he was able to keep his composure. They were led to a long table made from white marble and trimmed in gold. There were 20 seats ten on the right and ten on the left with a large seat at the head of it. Mr. Stanke and Wellington had been the first to arrive they were shown their seats. Both sat where they were told and waited. An eerie breeze of frigid air blew through every few minutes making it uncomfortable and hard to focus on anything else but the temperature. After a fifteen-minute wait more guests arrived. one couple looked like they were from the northeast parts of Africa however, their skin was very pale which confused Mr. Stanke. he thought to himself "they dress like their Arab, but the skin tones are quite off" the gentlemen wore a blue turban with a blue Thobe to match. his wife's face was covered with a blue Niqab that only revealed her forehead and eyes. She too had on a long blue dress. They both sat down and nodded toward Mr. Stanke and Wellington who returned the acknowledgment. Just then others come into the large white room. People from all over the world were represented. They were dressed in extravagant clothing and expensive jewels. They were of all shapes and ethnic backgrounds. No one conversed with anyone outside of who they arrived with. those who came by themselves sat quietly. They waited and chatted for an hour or so. then a line of waiters came out of two sets of doors on each side of the large room with silver treys. Each one carries an assortment of foods from all over the world.

The greeter who met Mr. Stanke and wellington tapped a silver triangle and the crowd grew silent. "You may dine," he said and turn to walk out. Classical music flooded the area which created an elegant festive mood as the waiters began placing food on each person's plate. everyone began eating all except for Wellington who had refused his meal. He watched as Mr. Stanke and the others shoved mounds of food into their mouths. fork and spoonful after, fork and spoonful.

This went on for a while until the glutenous carnival was interrupted by a frigid wind that terminated all motion. A chilling silence was once again blanketed the room. Suddenly a large door appeared in the middle of the wall at the back of the room. a secret department in plain sight. Then He walked in slowly, floating alongside the table sinisterly looking at every guest. he was eerily slender and seemed to be more dead than alive in appearance. his red eyes sunken deep into his ghostly white face. As cold as it was this man had on no shirt.

a row of blue gemstones that sat around his neck, draped down to the middle of his chest.

Once he reached the large chair that was pulled out for him by the waiters, he sat. a large glass was filled with a red substance too thick to be wine was poured into a large chalice. He reached for the glass lifted it to his mouth and drank as a single red stream dripped down from the corner of his mouth. He drank until the glass was empty. Wiping his chin and holding his hand out to be clean by the waiter standing to his left. He grinned wide and took a deep breath, "so why are we here" he asks in a low raspy voice. "Can anyone tell me why I have to summon you to my world?" the man in the blue turban spoke up confidently "well sir, the man said with an air of haughtiness, "it is you who summoned us, so it is you who must have the answer to your own question" the man in the blue turban sat back with a large grin. He felt that his display of bravery placed him above the other guest who was cowering in the boss's presence. The boss was silent he smiled at the man in the blue turban who took this as a sign of approval for his display and return the boss's grin. but the boss grinned even larger. The man smiled a bit larger matching the boss's smile. But then the boss's smile turned extremely large and grotesque as it distorted into a smile reminiscent of a jack o lantern on Halloween night. Some of the guests turn their faces from the horrid sight. One man grabbed his mouth to hold in the vomit leaping up from his gut. The man in the blue turban was frozen in fear, now realizing he had made a terrible mistake in speaking up. He cleared his throat and tried to apologize, but it was too late. A waiter stepped forward to the right of the man and repeatedly drove a large steak knife into the man's chest. Mr. Stanke counted at least 30 strikes as blood splashed in every direction. Everyone whimpered and scurried to wipe the splatter of blood from their clothing. The boss's face return to its normal less scary display. He looked around and simply said "wrong fucking answer" he continued my Name is Hsub, to you I am God I have been here in this realm looking for an evil people who tried to destroy my people a long time ago, but I revolted against the people and now I search for the remanence of their clan who hide here in this time and space. Mr. Stanke could not believe what he was hearing. he thought to himself "this mutha fucka is Insane. he wondered what he had gotten himself into?" just then Hsub, who had read Mr. Stanke's mind. turn to Mr. Stanke and said, "you've gotten yourself into a good place if you do what your told and don't disappoint me." He then asked, "do you understand me? you vicious piece of jelly" Mr. Stanke was terrified. He was so scared that he pissed on himself a little bit. he noticed Wellington was cool as a cucumber, so Mr. Stanke tried his best to regain his composure and put up a good front. Hsub then told his guest why they were there and the problem they had with the Rahsan people and how they were going to deal with it. The body of the man in the blue turban continued to rest motionless as his blood saturated the white tablecloth. He spoke about the plan to turn the Rahsan into dope fiends and slaves to his chemical. He spoke about his plan, and that it had worked but, in some places, the Rahsan were resisting his drugs and overthrowing the dealers, and this had to stop. "It's come to my attention that it has started in the North Oakland area of California where our colleague Mr. Stanke is in control." Hsub turned to Mr. Stanke and asked. "Mr. Stanke is this something you can't handle?" Mr. Stanke began to answer but was quickly cut off but Hsub "remember our friend's answer." (Motioning to the lifeless body of the man in the blue turban) he continued "please don't make the same mistake." Mr. Stanke remained silent. "I'm going to send you some muscle to help with this issue, it should be handled expeditiously," Hsub said with a deep hissing voice. "Do you understand?" Mr. Stanke nodded in the affirmative. "Good, now take yo' fat ass back to Cali" Mr. Stanke rose in a hurry and turned to walk out just as Hsub frowned in disgust as he caught a whiff of something foul "Goddam, did you shit yourself?" asked Hsub. turns out it was not just urine that Mr. Stanke released in his pants. Mr. Stanke and Wellington both exited the room with haste. The laughter of Hsub echoed in their ears all the way back to their hotel.

☀ ☀ ☀

Meanwhile back in Oakland. Everyone thanks the brothers for saving them from the clutches of their addiction. The word was out and the truth of who they began to flow through the community. As the days followed more and more people wanted to be down with the new righteous dope. all the major dealers quickly switch to serving John's supply. Those who still worked for Mr. Stanke began to see a decline in the demand for the poison they were used to putting out.

They reported back to Mr. Stanke Who was already under pressure from the big boss. But now he had devised a plan to stop John and his crew. He told his top lieutenants "Lower your prices and up the potency of the product." He explained, "we want every man woman, and child on every drug we sale!"

The lieutenants followed orders. They left all the dope, as pure as possible. The dope that was not strong enough was laced with fentanyl a deadly drug created in 1959 that has been used to kill off the Rahsan people. Somehow it has gotten into the other more affluent parts of town, so the government scaled it back.

Mr. Stanke was not taking any chances he wanted John stopped by any means necessary. he sent his meanest and most deadly troops to all the turfs in and around Oakland. Places like Richmond, San Francisco, Hayward, and South Berkeley which was a ancient hiding place for the Rahsan people. There were shootouts and brawls between Mr. Stanke's' henchmen and the new Rahsan army. For two years straight. Lives were being lost on both sides. However, the Rahsan army was more than prepared to do battle. they had been fighting against each other for decades not knowing who they were. But now they had a common enemy and coupled with the knowledge of self they easily began to smash the invaders and push them back out of the surrounding communities.

Mr. Stanke was losing the war, but the reinforcements were constantly being deployed. Hsub had been sickened by Mr. Stanke's inability to put down the uprisen of the Rahsan army. He feared that soon John would be led to the truth about his father and grandfather. Hsub called for his soldiers in the other realm to assemble on the earth plane, and ready themselves to attack. Little did Hsub know that his thoughts and fears were well-founded.

John, Uncle Sonnie, Jamal, dame, and Ed Roe all formed separate armies under their control. they had all the Bay Area, Sacramento, and L.A. turfs secure. John called a meeting at

Bushrod Park in North Oakland for all Rahsan. it was time to announce the ultimate plan.

The brothers and sisters flocked from all over California. The gathering was to be held at dawn thousands of beautiful black faces and glowing green eyes gathered greeting each other like long-lost family. the ancient love that was born millenniums ago flowed through the cosmic beating of each united heart causing a rhythm felt by all.

as the holy and righteous breath circulated in and out the lungs of the mighty Rahsan people. The sun began to rise as John ascended a makeshift platform and as the sun's light seized his body causing a penumbra around his form. John shouted out "behold your one and only creator, the great SAN!" the people cheered as the Sun rose even higher and brighter the reflection of light seem to reflect off the skin of the Rahsan, they all began to shimmer each projecting a golden hue from their skin. The vibratory frequency from their heartbeat became so high that they seem to fade out of regular eyesight. To bystanders, they looked like thousands of spirits gathered on "FET GEDE," and all was quiet. And for the first time in a millennium, they heard the Great SAN speak to them. They were clean and righteous and now able to receive the Holy Language of God.

"My children who have suffered, be not crestfallen by the experience of your lives, all that you have chosen to rise above was for a grand purpose. The all-divine purpose was to bring you here to this very moment in time. For it is here that you realize who you are. Not just Rahsan people, not just holy people, not just the chosen few, but the very existence of every particle in your makeup. Yes, Ye' are Eye and eye are Ye,' the great SAN continued "You are my eyes

to see, my ears to hear, my mouths to speak. I move through your limbs. I create myself out of your flesh. You are that eye' am"

Tears began to flow from the eyes of everyone including John and the crew they had not heard the voice until now, and they did not understand the truth of who they are. The great San continued *"My children you will be Saved by John the Pope"* The Rahsan began to dance and celebrate the coming of the great Mothership, the return of the one, the true reality of Hue-Man.

Now John spoke to the people "My brothers and sisters the time has come for us to take back what is rightfully ours Hsub made a grave mistake he thought he could create his own world and become the new great SAN. which led to his loss of membership in this universal family. He then thought by wiping out all Rahsan, that he and his Nashar would be able to destroy the great SAN. but like so many before him, he was mistaken. In a few days, we will Strike at Hsub. not only here on earth but in the other realms as well. Why in the other realms you asked. well because we have family and friends who we have lost to the Nashar, and they are being held captive. We must go there and free them. the enemy cannot defeat us because we are one." Then John shouted, "CAN YOU DIG IT?" to which the crowd responded in unison "DAM RIGHT!"

The great SAN had spoken to the people, and they received the information. Now they were truly blessed beyond their wildest dreams. the fight to rescue their loved ones from the clutches of the Nashar was the ultimate goal. The drums began and the Rahsan danced themselves into a trance state preparing for the war they called out to the great SAN for strength and courage. They could feel their destinies in their own hands for the first time in their lives.

XIII

Chapter 13

WAR IS HELL, BUT VICTORY IS BLISS.

The crew sat back overlooking the festivities they each had grown into powerful Wizards of their own right. Each perfecting a style all their own. While they watched and enjoyed the people Jamal looked over to dame and said, "Hey man, this is great and all, but we haven't seen nor heard from salamander in a while he continued what do you think he's been up to?" "I don't know man, shit maybe he figured we could take from here and don't need his help anymore." Jamal shakes his head in the negative and replies "shit dude, I still have a ton of unanswered questions. Just then ed roe leaned forward and yelled "ME TOO, GODDAMIT!" they all laughed. All except for sonny who was staring off into the distance.

He notices movement coming through the neighborhood. He squinted his eyes to get a better look. A large number of people were coming their way. Sonny stood up and was startled at the sight of an army getting ready to attack he yelled "they're here!" this caught John's attention, he ran to the makeshift podium screaming to the top of his lungs. "The enemy is upon us; may the great SAN hold us up" then all the Rahsan people turned toward the army who were outnumbered five to one and charged them ferociously.

The crew rushed to the front of the battle. Mr. Stanke had launched a full-on attack against the Rahsan. The battle was a slaughter the Rahsan ran through the oncoming forces as if they were children. Mr. Stanke's army was full of drug-filled, out-of-shape toxic-minded goons who ran on fear and negativity they had been totally cut off from the great San and turned out by the bad magic of Mr. Stanke's dope. The battle lasted for only twenty minutes. When it was all over the bodies of the Mr. Stanke army were laid out all over the Bushrod field.

Mr. Stanke stared in horror as the last of his soldiers spent their last breaths. He and Wellington watch on closed-circuit TV filmed from a camera set up on a telephone post. Mr. Stanke sat motionlessly. He clutched tightly to a glass of alcohol as the ice clang against the sides magnified by the utter silence. Sweat slipped down the sides of his fat bald head. His lips quivered from the jolting thoughts of punishment from Hsub.

Wellington smiled, "What the fucked are you smiling about you goddam imbecilic monkey, we are dead once Hsub gets word of our failure" Mr. Stanke screamed with unbridled consternation. "don't you understand? you and I are no more, finished" he continued. Then Wellington's Smile grew shrank into a frown. He turned slowly on the back of his heels in smooth motion he began to walk over to where his boss was seated and he to him soothingly "Mr. Bossman, we aren't dead yet there are a few loose ends that need to be explained."

"What are you talking about, what loose ends?" Mr. Stanke asked. Wellington stepped up behind his boss, placing his hand on his shoulders gently turning him to a large mirror. Then wellington spoke. "See Mr. S I have watched you for a long time. I have watched you when you did not even know I was watching you. I totally understand mutha fuckas like you. Your greed and insatiable appetite for money and power. You would sell your own Mammie for a hundred bucks if you were offered. I knew who you would be. A dirty, fat stinking piece of shit." Mr. Stake tried to interrupt with objection but was quickly silenced by a solid blow to the side of his head that caused him to bleed profusely. The red liquid ran down into his white suit. Mr. Stanke whimpered from the pain confused he managed to mutter "what are you doing I have treated you like a son wellington. How can you betray me?"

Wellington gently slide his hand under Mr. Stanke's chin and lifted his head to the mirror so his boss could see him in the Reflection. Then as Mr. Stanke watched in paralyzing fear, Wellington's face began to distort and after a few seconds, Mr. Stanke realized his fate. Wellington was Salamander in disguise the whole time. All his plots and plans were conceived in the presence of the enemy. Mr. Stanke in his greedy rage to poison the Bay Area had not realized that the man he had confided in for over twenty years had slightly changed. And an imposter had taken his place.

Mr. Stanke asked to know where the real wellington was, and when did he step in to take his place? Salamander's face cold and emotionless it has been 10 years since I killed your butler. Mr. Stanke's head dropped with sorrow. "But don't you worry your fat sweaty greedy big head" salamander continued as his hand slipped into his pocket and retrieved a syringe filled with heroin. before Mr. Stanke could make any attempt to refuse his destiny Salamander drove the needle into Mr. Stanke's neck and jammed down the plunger blasting the brown liquid into the vein of Stanke's blubbery neck.

Salamander took a step back as Stanke's body went limp. Stanke began to moan in pure ecstasy as the heroin crept through his veins. But just as he slipped into a blissful death, Salamander jumped onto the back of Stanke's chair wrapping a steel wire around his neck, and strangled him without remorse. As the wire sank deeper into the neck of Mr. Stanke, Salamander whisper to him "this is for all my people, when you get to the forbidden place create a space for your boss because he's going to join you shortly. you rotten disgusting piece of jelly. Salamander gave one more ferocious tug, severing the head of Stanke completely.

Salamander watched the fat round head fall and rolled a few feet coming to rest upside down. then he turned and walked over to the record player in the corner of the room. He bent down and thumbed through the collection until he reached Diana ross's 'The Boss.' album. He took the record out and blew the dust off. then placed it on the record player grabbing the needle he went to the song he wanted. The needle hit the surface of the record. "it's my house and I live here" Diana ross's voice blasted into the room, as Stanke's body slipped the floor with a loud thump. Salamander exited the room singing the lyrics closed the door behind him.

It was time to enter the final phase of his plan. He needed

to gather the crew and the rest of the army. 90% of the Rahsan people had been freed from the clutches of Mr. Stanke's dope. They were strong and focused on community building. They just needed to rescue their elders and set up the ancient family structure that was the backbone of their existence. God, family, and community were the natural order of things, and it was time for the elders to return to lead the way.

John, Jamal, Dame, ED roe, and Uncle Sunny were at the pink house strategizing their next move. When the faint vibration of the funk ruffled their concentration. As the funk grew stronger it became clear that the music was headed in their direction.

The brothers leaped to their feet and rushed to the door. To their delight was a fantastic sight the magic dazzling, distinguished dude had returned to fold. Salamander pulled his automobile up on the lawn as it sparkled in the sun's light. He floated from the driver's seat and slide up to the front door like a king python patrolling the jungle. "How do you do children? It is I the one and only, never could be a phony, master of the highest degree, chief in any pedigree and Grand sheik of the jubilee!"

then salamander tipped his hat to the brothers. He flung his long green cape to the side as he walked into the house. The brothers were happy to see salamander they had so many questions as to his whereabouts and they wanted to tell him about the battles they had won. they were all talking at once. Salamander waved his hand to calm his friends. He said "I know you are wondering where I have been and let me tell you. I was on an undercover mission to destroy our enemy from the inside. Mr. Stanke is no more." "Brothers" he continued "as a wizard of the highest order I can do things that you can only dream about. I can shapeshift and become whoever I want" salamander then transformed into Wellington. The brothers were stunned, and Jamal yell out "hey it's that fat dope dealer's, right-hand man!" John then chimed in saying "so you mean to tell me that you were with the fat man all this time?" salamander who at this time had changed back to his usual form. Answered "yes." he then explained that he had to infiltrate the organization to see how the operation worked.

He said "What I found out was that there was a multitude of low-level dealers who had made deals with Mr. Stanke. One such dealer was a dude you may be familiar with; he went by the name of spooky man."

John was frozen. The news of his closes friend conspiring with the Nashar was too much to handle. Salamander continued "spooky man was sent to you. the mission was to keep you high and depended on the dope so you could never develop into the wizard you were always meant to be. For a few years, it was working until spooky man changed his mind and decided to disobey his orders. He began by giving you less potent amounts of dope. This was how I was able to home in on your frequency. The dope you were being given was not ordinary Heroin, it was laced with a disruptive agent to change your Rahsan DNA. Spooky man was adding less and less of the agent, and Once I locked in on you Mr. Stanke sent the police to kill spooky man and make it look like he was at fault for his own demise." Salamander continued, "Detective Buttinsky was not just a detective, he was an agent of Mr. Stanke's Mob, and if you had agreed to lie on spooky man and say he had a gun your vibratory frequency would have been changed and you would have been lost to us forever." Salamander then said

"Please allow me to go deeper, when you sincerely asked the great San for help you sent up to him a powerful frequency that he magnified and then reverberated out across all the realms once the noblemen felt it, we knew it was time. Another battle was set in motion. So here we are." Then Dame asked, "so what now we have the armies, we are trained very well, when do we strike?"

Shiiid, my brother we attack now! Salamander said confidently and with a wave of his hand salamander had teleported the brothers to Bushrod Park. All the leaders were there Scooty-D, lil Jesse, E-Moseby the electric man, Toby-T, D-nice the sorceress and her daughter guided by her mother's Love, Uschold the Director, J-Dennis the trainer, Alisha the lioness and a host of others. All had gathered to help defeat the evils forces that have poisoned our worlds. Standing in the Void to make sure the future generations of Rahsan people will live free.

Tens of Thousands of Rahsan's waiting for the order to go into battle. The beating of a large drum was the signal to assume the position of meditation. The deep boom followed by a long pause settled the large army into a trance. The army began to sway back and forth to the slow beat. The waves of energy started to rise from the crowds. And so, it begins!

A plume of white energy arose from the sea of Rahsan warriors each leader stood in front of their platoons. John yelled attack and the entire army blasted into a hypersonic ball of energy.

The entire crowd flickered in and out of this reality. screams of pain escaped from some of the Rahsan who had not released all their false egos. the meditation was shifting their existence and ripping their positive minds from the Negative. "Only the pure can go into the battle and connect with ancestors," shouted salamander. let go of the falsehood you have been indoctrinated to think the negative is real. you are the Rahsan people you are more ancient than anything you can think of. let go of the idea of being a slave to the material things of this temporary life."

"We are going home to fight for our people trapped in the prisons of Hsub's unnatural irregular interdimensional toilet of negative thoughts," John shouted. "We are going into the universal subconscious mind's center to help the great San recalibrate its own design. this will liberate our ancestors and allow them to live with us and guild us forever." John said.

Suddenly they were all gone. Bushrod Park was empty.

Darkness, silence. Complete and utter emptiness engulfed the army. They had become pure thought in the middle of the universal subconscious mind, where worlds are birth into existence. Where there is no self. The beginning and the end simultaneously, the above and below intertwined Here time does not exist. There are only possibilities born as reflections of the thought manifested from a single point.

They have become one cell of energy vibrating recreating creation, growing in the emptiness. Until a great explosion, an atomic burst of energy that blasted forth, and now the army is made of material again. But this time they are not in the subconscious, they are in the realm of Hsub's prison face to face with the Nashar army.

Salamander stared across at his enemy as the Glowing red eyes of Hsub peered back. They spoke to one another telepathically "so we meet again my old nemesis" Hsub said annoyed. Salamander's reply was just as condescending. "Some hoes are hard to get rid of and you're a hoe that just won't leave." Hsub paused for long while and then spoke again "you may have been able to save Raheem, but the rest of the Rahsan will never be set free. I have infected their subconscious minds and it would take thousands of Salamanders or should I say willie sharps to undo the damage. So, you see you have lost the war already. These small skirmishes will not make any difference, no one can escape." Salamander's sinister laugh echoed throughout the darkness. "You have not won anything. you are temporary! fleeting energy dissipating with every awakening of the Rahsan people. John has been wakened and along with him, thousands of others" replied Salamander. Just then John rose from darkness "your dope game is over!" your underlings are dead and those who still have breath, have been removed from the Rahsan communities." John continued "we are here to reclaim the ancestors and to free my father and grandfather. So, hand them over Hsub." there was a long silence then Hsub Laughed and shouted, "Once again Willie Sharp has led a young fool into battle under false illusions, your father and grandfather aren't alive in the sense of being able to return to the living, you young dummy!" Hsub continued to laugh. John turned to salamander.

Salamander grinned slightly and spoke: "My name is Willie Sharp, to you I am Salamander. I am a guide to the inner self for my people. I lead you back to the poisonous seed planted in your minds when you are young. I help you get there and reevaluate your experience. that is my only duty as a nobleman. I have trained you; I have guided you. Now you must discern your path from here." Salamander fell silent. John stared at his conductor who had guided him to this moment, salamander also known as Willie Sharp. His eyes became piercing pools of confusion. John became lost, he was mentally unsure of what he was supposed to do next. Who could he trust? He questioned who he was at that moment. Shout from the warriors in the darkness began to be heard they encouraged john to seek his truth and rely on the great SAN for guidance.

John quivered with anger. He questioned his mission; he relived all the degrading days of drug abuse. A myriad of thoughts bounced off his skull, like a mentally ill man charging the white walls in his padded room. he had gotten into drugs, to hide from the pain of his father's death. at that time, he was susceptible to the bad influence of his friend spooky man. John had lost his hero, and he needed something to replace the deep dark void. Once on the drugs, the menacing monkey metamorphosized from the need to hide from the enfeebling trauma of losing his father to being a self-imagined disappointment to him.

He always figured his father was looking down on him in disgust. This only made him want to go deeper and bask in the false world weaved by the white horse galloping through his Veins. John cringed at the memories of horrifying ecstasy. He could feel the wetness of the blood between his fingernails, as he remembered scratching himself raw.

there was a moment of silence and then suddenly John remembered his training and he began to recalibrate his thinking. he thought from a different angle. Spooky man had made a mistake and tried to reconcile by giving him of lesser amount of poison. Spooky man changed his course for the better and he died a good guy. John continued to go deeper he pondered that he had also gotten off the dope in the hope that he could redeem himself in his father's eyes. He himself had decided to change course. The prospect of seeing his father again was so strong, that it freed him from the clutches of the dope world. his father's death manifested the birthplace of a million possibilities. how was he to respond to it? he could be negative and self-destructive, or he could be righteous and creative. He could help others to deal with the tragedy of losing a parent or close loved one. He had once chosen wrong and nowhere was a chance to re-cast himself as the hero and not the villain.

John was beginning to understand: *"One reaction leads to damnation and the other leads to salvation both choices spawned from the one experience."* Hsub uses the experience by cultivating negative reactions to the experiences. He preys on the youth because their minds are more susceptible to negative influences after a tragedy. Tragedies that his system of life creates. The young Rahsan are at risk because they lack the reasoning power to cope with tragedy. Their world turns grey, and then Hsub's henchmen supply drugs that provide a false color. Hsub plants the seed and guilds the young up the rocky concrete hill of perdition only to have them cast their souls into the pit of a hellish false reality.

John had gained an understanding of his plight. Mungu and his father were not trapped by Hsub. Their souls were trapped by John himself. His negative choices after his father's death were the cage, that encased their souls. John kept his ancestors from helping him in life by blocking the universal subconscious connection. No one really dies they leave this physical dwelling to flow in the everlasting spring of energy connected to their offspring forevermore. John understood that he was his ancestors, and he could commune with them anytime he wanted.

John raised his hand, and the entire Rahsan army stood to attention. Hsub scoff at the display and nodded to his followers. They rose to the challenge and prepared for battle. A moment of silence. then the command of Love was given by John and the two forces collided with each other causing a ripple effect throughout the Darkness of Hsub's false plain. Which affected the universal subconscious mind's vibratory frequency and all in existence. The other realms, the organic make-up of all People, flowers, animals, landscapes, and elemental reality began to flicker and shift. Changing colors and shapes as the battle between positivity and negativity swayed in the balance. the days fast-forwarded and then slowed to a snail's pace. Both sides fought viciously each soldier carrying the positive or negative spark that could change the outcome of the war. the two sides fought each other viciously receiving small victories as time stopped and Studded. Until a large boom was heard, and a new warrior rose out of the Rahsan side. This young brave warrior began to slash through the Nashar soldiers like lava through the plastic bags. John was amazed by this new guy on the battlefield, but something was oddly familiar about this person John was busy fighting his battle, but he kept looking at the valiant warrior. Then it hit him, it was Robert T. but he was younger than what

John had remembered. Just then as Robert T. slashed through a nashars chest with his mighty sword he looked over at John and winked. Then he went back to the battle and disappeared into the crowd of fighters. Nashar began to fall in the hundreds. the positive new thought was contagious and spread rapidly throughout the Rahsan. Hsub realizing he was again losing a battle quickly turned his tactics to the individual leaders. He sent mental seeds to distract them. he sent a wave of self-doubt confusing the leaders which slowed them down. Earl the electric man was struck with a heavy blow that broke his heart. one of Hsub's soldiers had struck down one of Earl's sons. But with help of his warrior queen Nafeesah by his side, they were able to create a new thought, which led to a new blessing. With the help of the great San, they both quickly remembered that no one ever really dies and that their son lives on within them and their other children. this knowledge allowed them to carry on with the fight of liberating the minds of our people. All the leaders had been sent obstacles that hurt or slowed them down, the illusion of death, low self-images, drug abuse, mental illness, and loneliness but the leaders were now in tune with the great San, and nothing could turn them back. They were "turnt-up" And ready.

The leaders quickly regained their composure and resumed the fight for positivity and mental freedom. Hsub retreated, and he began searching for another dimension. He thought of another timeline that could possibly stop Willie Sharp from awakening another pupil. He conjured a hole in the mental fabric of the universal subconscious mind he saw a place and time in 1952 in the city of Gaston Alabama. Hsub walked into the portal as the Nashar army was defeated. Willie Seeing where Hsub had gone quickly created his own portal and went through it in pursuit of his enemy. By this time, the last Nashar had been vanquished, and the battle had been won. The Rahsan stood together in victory and all raised their fist to solute John.

John, along with uncle sonny, Dame, Jamal, and Ed roe had learned the ways of the ancient Rahsan people. They had turned the northside of Oakland into a haven for all Rahsan people all over the world. Bushrod park has become the head-quarters for the new resistance. We now have A flourishing and beautiful Drug-free, community Where the young Rah-san is taught the skills to keep the negative mind tricks of Hsub and the Nashar soldiers out. Healthy communication between all the tribe leaders of Oakland has been established to keep love and respect throughout our streets. New Rahsan wizards are being trained and sent off to other dimensions to establish other safe zones. The war is turning. The Rahsan is on the Move.

At this moment blissfulness is king in the universal sub-conscious mind of the great San. As John sits atop his 68' Fal-cons. his legs crossed over the other. his spinal column erected and with eyes closed. he meditates intensely. He can feel the cool breeze flow over the bridge of his nose. Gently lifting the tiny hairs of his eyebrows, the slight thud of his slow beating heart creates the mystical rhythm on this journey of solitude. John no longer missed his father or grandfather because in these moments he could talk to them and receive the insight and instructions needed to carry on, and this wisdom can be passed down forever and evermore.

he was Free, and the city was saved by John Da Pope.

And so, it is...

The End

☼

Robert Thurston Hankins Jr is an African American author born and raised in North Oakland, CA. His mission is to reintroduce the world through literature to the majestic beauty, mystic insights, and the significance of the philosophies in African American culture. He wants all readers, no matter their background, to open their minds and enjoy his writing. The reader gets to engage in a different world from their own perspective. You don't always have to understand the language to enjoy it. Take in the linguistic vibration and enjoy the ride. Mr. Hankins' "Live your Dreams" attitude is featured throughout his work. There is a deep lesson in perseverance in his writing. Mr. Hankins started writing books using just his smartphone's notepad while working as security in San Francisco's busy union square financial district which is an adventure unto itself. Mr. Hankins was determined to become a Published Author, and by using the principles he learned as a young man, he was able to turn his life story into a novel that will make you laugh, cry, and root for the Hero and other characters on this journey.

www.ingramcontent.com/pod-product-compliance
Lightning Source LLC
Chambersburg PA
CBHW022214050726
47590CB00002B/797